Bolan hit hard ground at thirty-five miles per hour

He came out of a shoulder roll, but momentum catapulted him over the side of an embankment. He plunged through bushes that covered the slope and finally came to rest on his back at the foot of a wooden fence.

Ortiz and his hardmen leaped from the Volvo, intent on recovering their prisoner. The drug lord shouted a string of orders, and his men began to fan out and descend the slope, their weapons up and probing for a target.

A screech of brakes signaled a new arrival. A tall thin American got out of a Mercedes and strode over to Ortiz. Bolan couldn't hear the conversation, but they seemed to be arguing. Suddenly the drug dealer and his men returned to their vehicle, got in and drove away.

With a start of surprise, Bolan realized that he knew his savior. What had started out as a routine mission had just taken on a bizarre twist. What was a former rich kid from Philadelphia doing in the mountains of Colombia?

MACK BOLAN®

The Executioner

DON PENDLETON'S
THE EXECUTIONER®
FEATURING MACK BOLAN®

HELLDUST CRUISE

A GOLD EAGLE BOOK FROM
WORLDWIDE®

TORONTO • NEW YORK • LONDON • PARIS
AMSTERDAM • STOCKHOLM • HAMBURG
ATHENS • MILAN • TOKYO • SYDNEY

First edition November 1990

ISBN 0-373-61143-9

Special thanks and acknowledgment to
Peter Leslie for his contribution to this work.

The belief in a supernatural source of evil is not necessary; men alone are quite capable of every wickedness.

—Joseph Conrad
1857–1924

The only thing necessary for the triumph of evil is for good men to do nothing.

—Edmund Burke
1729–1797

I've fought evil every step of the way, and there seems to be no end to it. The drug trade is as vile as it gets. Everyone has to do his part to try to stem the tide—before it engulfs us.

—Mack Bolan

To the ceaseless efforts
of the men and women of the DEA

PROLOGUE

A fleshy blonde showing too much cleavage sat next to the husky American at the wheel of the red convertible. The car swept past Rafael Mendoza on his mule, then braked for the first of the hairpins leading down the mountainside to the main highway and to Medellín.

The old man turned and watched it out of sight around a shoulder of the barren rock face. Plenty of people drove up here in expensive automobiles at weekends—drug barons, overseers from the mines, rich Colombians with upland ranches—but it was unusual to see Americans so far from the tourist water holes. He listened to the squeal of tires and the rising bellow of the exhaust as the convertible accelerated away from the corner; then he transferred his gaze to the brush-covered slope dropping away below. Presently the car reappeared on a loop of road far beneath him, its bodywork winking in the bright light as the driver laid down rubber, arrowing toward the last of the curves.

Sixty feet below the stone parapet guarding that bend, the broad ribbon of the highway bisected the valley. And just beyond the corner, hidden from the foreigners in the low-slung sports car but clearly visible to Rafael Mendoza, an ancient truck laden with crates of fruit was blocking the roadway. Evidently the trucker had found himself on the wrong road; now he was laboriously turning his decrepit vehicle.

The convertible entered the last hairpin too fast. Mendoza saw its brake lights blaze red. The car slewed sideways, was expertly corrected and snaked out of the bend—to find the way almost completely obstructed by the maneuvering truck.

Again the twin lights glowed. Then the American, realizing that he hadn't a hope in hell of stopping in time, wrenched the wheel in a desperate attempt to squeeze between the parapet and the truck's tailgate.

But the convertible, already partly out of control, lurched sideways again and slammed into the low stone wall.

Horror-struck, Mendoza watched helplessly as it burst through the parapet, rose into the air, to plunge out of sight onto the slant of rock linking the mountain road with the highway below. The trucker leaped from his cab and ran toward the cloud of dust mushrooming up over the shattered wall.

"WILL THEY LIVE?" the police captain asked the hospital intern. The young doctor raised white-jacketed shoulders in a shrug. "Barring complications," he said. "It was fortunate for them that it was an open car. They were both flung clear before it crashed on the rock."

"And their injuries?"

"Multiple contusions and extensive lacerations in each case. The man broke both legs against the wheel as he came out. But the woman is really worse off. There were boulders among the scrub where she landed. She suffered a fractured skull, a fractured pelvis and several broken ribs." He shook his head sadly. "It'll be some months before she'll be fully recovered."

The policeman frowned. He didn't like to think of his cases as human beings; they were numbers on a file. "They're still both unconscious?" he asked primly.

"And likely to remain so for some time. It was more than thirty minutes before the ambulance got to them, and the sun is fierce at that time in the afternoon."

"All afternoon, this time of the year," the captain replied. He sighed, flicking a speck of dust from the sleeve of his uniform. "I suppose we must go through the motions. I'll have to make a report, advise relatives and so on. Shall we look at their effects?"

The intern nodded and led the way to a waiting room at the far end of the hospital corridor. A highway patrolman sprang to attention as the two men entered. Behind him, the sounds of suburban traffic, a distant ambulance siren, filtered through green shutters closing out the dusk.

"Ah, Torres," the captain acknowledged. "What have we discovered about these unfortunate strangers?"

The man looked uncomfortable. "Captain," he said hesitantly, "I am very sorry, but . . . well, there is nothing. Nothing at all."

"Nothing? What about names, addresses?"

Torres shook his head slowly. "Nothing," he repeated. "No passports, no letters, no credit cards, no driver's license or insurance certificate on the man. No papers at all."

"But they're Americans, aren't they?"

"I believe so, but so far I haven't been able to make positive identification."

"You've contacted the embassy in Bogotá, of course?"

"Yes, sir. Nobody is missing."

The captain stared in disbelief. "That is very curious," he said at last. "Come, we will see if perhaps their clothes..."

He moved across the room to a table strewn with a billfold, a woman's purse and its contents, a pair of shattered sunglasses, shoes, tourist maps, a guide to nightlife in Bogotá and two piles of bloodstained clothing.

"I'm afraid we had to cut the garments," the young doctor began. "To get them off, you see. It was—"

"It doesn't matter," the policeman cut in. He picked up the ripped material and examined each item: a brightly colored silk shirt, underclothes, a skirt, what had been a pair of white jeans. Finally he dropped the last one back on the table and turned to the intern. "The man is right," he said. "This is very odd. Even the store labels and the makers' names have been removed."

The intern looked suitably impressed. "What does that suggest to you?" the captain said to Torres.

The patrolman cleared his throat. "The victims of the accident wished to remain anonymous?" he offered.

"Of course. And?"

"Because of that, one might assume that they were criminals?"

"Exactly."

The captain stirred the collection of savaged garments with a forefinger. "Foreign crooks in Colombia," he observed. "That spells drugs to me. You better turn this stuff over to the lab boys, see what they can dig up. And have them fingerprint both Americans. If we fax the prints and dental details to Washington, we could save ourselves a lot of trouble identifying these characters."

"Yes, sir."

"Meanwhile, what can witnesses tell us about the accident itself?"

"There were witnesses in three different cars on the highway," Torres said. "But all they saw was the convertible bounce down the rock slope after it crashed through the parapet."

The captain raised his eyebrows. "There were no witnesses up there?"

"We have found none."

"But good God, man, something must have caused the accident! *Why* did the car break through that parapet?"

Torres shrugged. "We could find no reason. There were two skid marks just after the last hairpin, about sixty yards from the breach in the wall—as though someone had braked hard there. But of course they could have been made by some other car. Those are dangerous curves if you don't know the road."

"Agreed. So, other than the broken wall, there are no marks at all where the car left the road?"

"No, Captain. None at all."

"This affair begins to puzzle me. So what about the car?"

"It was a four-seat convertible, a Maserati Kamsin," Torres said enviously. "A beautiful vehicle. It's completely wrecked, beyond any hope of repair."

"Yes, yes, but what about the license plates? Where did the car come from? Who's the owner? What was there of interest inside?"

Torres shook his head. "Another blank, sir. There was a Japanese transistor radio, an aerosol for cleaning the windshield, a pair of string gloves in the glove compartment, brandy in a flask that was smashed inside the door pocket. No papers."

"And the owner's name?"

"The car was rented, Captain. Locally registered and hired from a garage in Manizales."

"Ah. Then the rental company should be able to give us a line."

"Yes, sir. Pasquale is over there now, making inquiries."

But the rental company was unable to supply them with names; the papers had been signed on behalf of an organization.

"S-A-F-E?" the police captain read out slowly in his office the following morning. "What the hell does that stand for? Is it some damned religious cult?"

"Not exactly," the patrolman named Pasquale told him. "It's an American organization all right. Kind of a welfare group. The letters mean . . ." He consulted a page torn from his notebook. "They stand for Save America from Evil. Evil in this case being drugs."

"They sure came to the right place," the captain grunted. "But I never heard of these people. Do they have an office in the city?"

"SAFE is a clean-up social group, funded by a millionaire trust. They also do what the Americans call good works—looking after earthquake survivors, helping the victims of famine, floods and like that."

"We have no famine and no floods in Medellín."

"No, sir. We don't have a SAFE office, either."

"Perhaps it is just as well." The captain eased his collar away from his neck with a damp finger. It was stuffy in his office. "Did anyone think to check out the mileage on the car's odometer against the figures logged by the garage when it was rented?"

Pasquale's plump cheeks bunched in a self-satisfied smile. "Yes, Captain. I got the figures from the rental clerk this morning and then went to look at the wreck. The Maserati had covered more than twelve hundred miles since it was rented three days ago."

"Ha! With no passports they couldn't have crossed any frontiers. Let's take a look." The captain rose from his desk, removed his jacket and draped it over the back of his chair, then picked up an outsize pair of wooden dividers and walked to a wall map. The ceiling fan in that corner of the room stirred the hot, heavy air and detached a tendril of hair from his carefully groomed head as he applied the points of the dividers to the scale. "Yes," he said a moment later, "as I thought—they could have crossed the Cordilleras and made a round trip to the Brazilian border. They could have covered the whole coast, through Cartagena and Barranquilla to La Guajira on the Caribbean side, and down past Cali to Tumaco on the Pacific. Or, for that matter, made many small trips locally. Contact our people in those cities and ask if *they* have any mission or bureau operated by this foreign organization."

"Yes, sir."

The officer sat down at his desk again. "I'm not happy with this lack of witnesses. Surely somebody must have seen what happened. It's a busy road. Put out a radio call—an accident occurred, a red sports car left the road, two foreigners were gravely injured, will anyone who saw the tragedy please contact... You know the drill.''

"Very well, Captain."

"Perhaps this matter will automatically clarify itself once we know who the victims are."

1

"Harvey Lee?" Mack Bolan repeated. "Yeah, I know him slightly. Used to work for the Company. What was he doing in Colombia—helping out DEA?"

"I wish we knew," Hal Brognola replied. "He still free-lances for Langley, maybe a couple times a year. But this time he was working for us, checking out one of the Hispanic connections in Florida."

"And then you hear he's been found under a wrecked Maserati in Colombia."

Brognola sighed. "That's it. And we wouldn't even have been wise to that if it hadn't been for this signal from Bogotá, asking for a trace based on prints and dental details. Clearly he's chasing up some narcotics angle, but he hasn't filled us in on one damn thing. That's what I can't understand."

Bolan shrugged. "Maybe he had a good hand, figured he'd score better if he played it close to the vest. Was the car sabotaged?"

"Negative—according to the local law. But it seems there were things about the accident that had them guessing."

"And you reckoned it might be a good idea to have someone who wasn't part of the hired help start digging around a little?" Bolan queried.

"You got it." Brognola, the rumpled, tired-looking Justice Department Fed who bossed the NSA's Sensitive Operations Group, had been Bolan's link with the Oval Office when the big man had worked secretly for Uncle Sam. Now Bolan himself was free-lance, dispensing his own brand of justice. But the two men kept in touch. And sometimes, in cases *too* sensitive for the department to be openly involved, Bolan was still called in unofficially to help.

In cases like this one, for example.

"The Administration sweats blood trying to keep on good terms with the Colombians," Brognola explained. "Especially when three-fourths of the drugs flooding the U.S. originate there, and the damn country's practically run by the big Medellín cartel. We can't risk sending in an official investigator on this Harvey Lee thing. It could screw up a dozen different cases if the Colombians took offense and refused to play ball."

"What do you want me to do?" the warrior asked.

The two men were standing at the window of Brognola's office in Washington, D.C., looking down at the stream of traffic snarled up in Eleventh Street's noonday rush. Rain beat against the windowpanes and polished the roofs of the honking cars, trucks and taxis below.

"Several things," Brognola replied. "Find out if the accident *was* an accident, why Lee quit Florida, what exact trail led him to Colombia, and ask him, too, why the hell he kept us in the dark, why the screwball change of image."

"Screwball?"

"You know Harvey. He's an Ivy League specimen. Brooks Brothers suit with a button-down collar and a necktie. He works normally under some kind of executive cover, doesn't talk with anyone below the rank of ambassador. Except that this time he was dressed down, real casual, sported a droopy mustache, and was traveling with a beautiful blonde from Vegas with enough vice convictions to fill a Law Society journal.''

Brognola turned back into the room and walked to his desk. He picked up a sheet of paper. ''You know as well as I do, Striker, that ain't Harvey's style. And there's one thing more.'' He glanced at the paper. ''At the time of the accident he was flashing a gold tooth and the dental records show that this crown has to be fitted over a perfectly sound incisor. How do you read that?''

''I'd say he was building a solid cover, to hide his regular cover,'' Bolan replied.

''So would I, and I'd sure as hell like to know why.''

Mack Bolan, a.k.a. the Executioner, swung his muscled six-foot-three-inch frame away from the window as a gust of wind flung a scatter of raindrops against the glass. ''They tell me the Pacific beaches are just dandy this time of year. Maybe I should take a South American vacation—and start asking a few questions.''

PALM TREES LINED the private road leading to the hospital and shaded the verandas that surrounded the low white building. From the steps rising to the visitors' entrance, soaring apartment buildings could be seen over the oleander hedge enclosing the property farther down the hill. Bolan brought the rented Toyota to a stop on the graveled driveway, strode up the steps and pushed through revolving doors into the reception lobby.

A large pendant fan spun slowly in the shadowy entrance. Beneath it a uniformed police officer was talking to a young woman seated at a desk. Under her starched hospital cap, the woman flashed a professionally inquiring smile at the Executioner. Bolan placed a briefcase on the desk and leaned forward. "Michael Belasko," he said in Spanish, "from New York. I'm an attorney delegated to represent two patients here—Miss Shirley Williams and Mr. Joe Sercondini, the Americans injured in the car accident. Are they conscious yet? Perhaps you'd be kind enough to direct me to their rooms."

The policeman had turned to stare curiously at Bolan. His sallow face was creased with fatigue. As the receptionist was about to speak, he cut in, "Captain Fernandez at your service, Counsellor." He held out his hand. "Clearly you haven't heard."

"Heard?" Bolan repeated, shaking the hand. "Heard what?"

"Both the patients are dead," the woman said.

"Dead? But I was told they were—"

"Yes, they were improving, both of them, though it's true that neither had recovered consciousness. But then..." The woman glanced hesitantly at Fernandez.

"Regrettably, most regrettably, there seems to have been those with an interest in seeing that they never did recover consciousness," the police officer supplied.

"They were murdered?"

"Unfortunately. We might very well have accepted that your clients—who were believed to be criminals— had succumbed to their injuries. But the intruder or intruders left open a window that should have been closed, and once we became suspicious we asked the postmortem pathologist to keep—how do you say?— the open eye."

"And he found?"

"He found, beyond all doubt, that the patients had been killed by that simplest of all methods—an air bubble injected straight into a vein by means of a hypodermic syringe.''

"That," Bolan said, "is the clincher. You're saying this couple were players on the drug scene?''

Captain Fernandez spread his arms. "Who knows? In this country, what other scenes are there? It was just that with the deliberate removal of all personal identification, it seemed the couple had something to hide.''

"I understand," Bolan said. He was unwilling at that stage to reveal that Harvey Lee—whose name had been passed on by the FBI as Sercondini—was in fact working for the U.S. Department of Justice.

Later, in the captain's downtown office, he asked, "As a lawyer, of course, I have no right to question you, but, purely as a matter of interest, do you have any idea why these people were killed? Or who was responsible?''

"None, Counsellor. At the same time—purely as a matter of interest, of course—I'm curious to know how this unfortunate couple contrived to instruct a lawyer to come all the way from New York to represent them...when in fact they never recovered consciousness after the accident. An accident, presumably, they never knew had occurred.'' The officer's stare was expressionless.

Bolan smiled. "My bad Spanish. I said I was *delegated* to represent them. I wasn't of course instructed by the victims. That would, as you say, have been impossible. My briefing,'' he said, "was from the SAFE headquarters. Neither of the victims belonged, or was in any way connected with the organization, and the directors want to know what the heck is going on.''

"And you hoped to find out by questioning them? What would be called, in your language, a watching brief?"

"You could say that. Anything you could tell me, therefore, would be a great help."

"There is very little," Fernandez said tiredly. "The car was rented on behalf of the organization. No names were given, but the papers and indemnities they produced, all on official SAFE paper, appeared to be in order. They left a large cash deposit."

"Was the accident due to sabotage?"

"We think not. No direct witnesses came forward, but after putting out a radio message we pulled in a trucker who seems to have been the unwitting cause of it. The man had taken the wrong road and was making an illegal turn just before a sharp bend. He says the car came around much too fast, then hit the wall and went over, trying to avoid him."

"Why didn't he come forward at the time?"

"Usual reason. He thought he would be blamed, and he was right. The law is specific. It's forbidden—" Suddenly the official policeman, the captain cleared his throat self-consciously, then continued. "He'll be dealt with later. Meanwhile his testimony—"

"The car was coming down from the mountains?" Bolan interrupted. "You haven't found out where it was coming from, where these people were based?"

"Not yet. It's a big country, with many different regions beyond the Andes. We shall certainly find out in time."

"Sure," Bolan agreed. "In time. Right now my money says they were killed, once the accident had taken place, to delay inquiries into where they did come from. Are you with me, Captain?"

"But certainly. There is of course the possibility that papers and other forms of ID were removed from the bodies before the police or the ambulance crew arrived at the wreck, and not previously by the victims themselves."

Bolan nodded. "That had occurred to me. If you don't know who they are and where they came from, it's kind of tough tying them in with anything. So far," he said untruthfully, "we don't even know what business these people were in or why they were here."

"Your suggestion that they were in some way associated with the drug barons..." Fernandez began. Then he broke off in midsentence: one of the phones on his desk was buzzing.

He snatched it up and barked his name.

For a moment he listened, and then exclaimed, "You have to be joking!"

Holding the receiver against his chest, he stared at the Executioner. "The truck driver," he said blankly, "was found in a garbage dump outside the city with his throat cut."

2

Bolan called Hal Brognola from the central telegraph office in Medellín and was careful to phrase his report on the death of Harvey Lee and his companion in very general terms. "I think I found an honest policeman," he said when he had added the news about the trucker. "The guy has that haggard look cops wear when they know they aren't getting anyplace. Cops on the make are usually fat cats, all smiles with a can-I-help-you-sir attitude. Which they don't."

"Watch your step, Striker," the big Fed advised. "The guys behind the drug business are bad news. You know that as well as I do. Starting off next to Honest Joe may already have you tabbed as future dogmeat."

"I know it," the Executioner replied. "But I also know the scenario. I'm watching. And I'll call you when I get the intel. It may be a little while. My cover's under suspicion already."

"Just answer my three questions," Brognola said. "Once we know what Harvey was into, we can decide how to handle the cleanup from this end."

"It may take some time," Bolan repeated. "I suspect things are kind of sewn up in the territory Harvey was working."

He left the telegraph office and went back to his rented Toyota. It was parked seventy yards away at a meter flanking the sidewalk. The late-afternoon sun was still uncomfortably hot. Bolan figured on resting a couple hours before he started backtracking the mountain route taken by Harvey Lee's Maserati.

The road was jammed solid each way because a delivery truck loaded with crates of tequila had double-parked outside the liquor store across the street. Bolan threaded his way between the stalled vehicles, feeling in his pocket for the keys to the sedan.

He stepped up onto the sidewalk, slid the key into the lock on the driver's door and twisted.

The door of the delivery truck's cab swung open and the driver clambered down into the street, ignoring the angry shouts and blasting horns from the motorists blocked on either side. As the door moved, the outside mirror caught a shaft of sunlight and flashed a reflection across the road and through the Toyota's windshield.

Bolan's thumb was on the button that opened the door when the bright ray swept over the seat backs and illuminated a loop of wire dropping into the shadow beneath the seat of the Executioner's side of the car—a loop that hadn't been there when he parked the Toyota and locked the door.

Bolan's instinctive reactions to danger, honed razor-sharp in half a lifetime of jungle combat and guerrilla warfare, were lightning fast. A catlike leap projected him to the rear of the sedan, and he was flat on his face in the road when the detonation rocked the street.

The bomb must have been activated by a trembler coil with a ten-or fifteen-second delay, rather than a direct-contact breaker when the key was twisted in the lock. It was a relatively small charge—perhaps a pound of plastique beneath the driver's seat, with wires leading to a fusing device in the trunk and then back to the lock mechanism. If Bolan had opened the door and climbed into the car it would have erupted as he settled into the seat.

The flash of the explosion momentarily dimmed the sunlight as it blew out the glass, mangled the hood and punched open the roof of the vehicle. Hundredths of a second later the concussion had shattered half the windows in the block and pulverized most of the shop-front displays.

After an instant's shocked silence the street echoed with shouts, screams, the clatter of running feet. When the smoke cleared, the wrecked Toyota was slewed across the street with flames streaming from under the hood and the interior. The driver's door had been blown off and wrapped around the warped stem of a parking meter. The car in front lay on its side with one rear tire on fire.

Bolan sprawled on the ground, surrounded by debris. His face was blackened, he'd lost a little hair and his right shoe and sock had vanished. The sole of the bare foot was bleeding, but otherwise he appeared to be uninjured. He pushed himself to his hands and knees, then stood.

The street was full of people. Several of the drivers trapped in the traffic jam had been cut by flying glass. The delivery truck and a dozen automobiles had been damaged by the blast. In front of the liquor store, waiters from a nearby seafood restaurant gathered around a bloodied bundle that heaved spasmodically on the sidewalk: the delivery man had caught the full force of the explosion as he clambered over the tailgate of his truck.

Shaking his head to clear the ringing in his ears caused by the concussion, Bolan heard the angry voices around him.

"Another damned car bomb—when will it end?"

"I saw it go up. I was sitting at the wheel . . ."

"It's the drug dealers again. They should all be shot."

"Are you all right?" a woman asked Bolan. "You should sit down and take it easy until the ambulance comes. Really, it's monstrous—no one is safe anywhere these days."

"Thank you," Bolan said. "Thank you, I'm all right. It probably looks worse than it is."

Over the rumble of city traffic, he could hear the whistling scream of approaching patrol cars. As the driver of the booby-trapped car, the warrior figured it would be smart to leave the scene before a barrage of questions blocked him for the rest of the day. And maybe half the night. He slipped unobtrusively into a side street and limped away.

BOLAN HADN'T TOLD anyone that he was going to the telegraph office. The fact that his car had been sabotaged while he was in there had to mean, therefore, that he'd been tailed from his hotel.

A number of people knew that a New York attorney named Belasko was in town. Only two—the police captain and the receptionist at the hospital—knew that Belasko was interested in the accident victims. And was, by inference, an investigator whose mouth had to be closed, a piece to be swept from the board.

Clearly, whatever Harvey Lee had been into was ultrasensitive.

On a hunch, Bolan decided to hand Captain Fernandez a clean sheet at least to begin with, and check out the girl. He rented another car from a different agency in the name of Blanski, a second alias he had used a number of times before. According to his ID, Mr. Blanski was a realtor from Palm Beach, Florida, in Colombia on the lookout for properties that could be developed as vacation centers.

He parked the new car, a Spanish SEAT, in view of the hospital exit and settled down behind the wheel with a newspaper. Soon after eight o'clock small cars, a scooter, several young women on foot, began streaming out past the open gates as the day-shift nurses went home and the night shift came on duty. Ten minutes later, peering over the top of his paper, Bolan recognized the receptionist. She was walking fast. Fifty yards down the road, she turned into a small public park and hurried along the asphalt path. Bolan slipped out of the car and padded after her.

The path ran between bright banks of flowers turned greenish in the lamplight. At the far end, where a secondary branch led to a side exit, a tall broad-leaved tree blanketed the pathway with shadow. Bolan glanced swiftly behind him. There was nobody else in sight.

When she reached the center of the shadowed stretch, he pounced.

From behind, he encircled her neck with one hard arm. "One move, one sound, and I'll cut off your wind," he threatened.

The girl stiffened and stifled a scream. "Don't hurt me, don't hurt me," she pleaded in a shrill whisper. "Here, take this. It's all I've got!" She moved to hand him the shoulder bag.

"The money doesn't interest me. It's information I want." Bolan spun her around to face him.

"W-what do you want to know?" she gasped. Then, recognizing him as the New York attorney who had been interested in the murdered accident victims, her eyes widened even more and she added in a weak voice. "Why are you . . . ? I m-m-mean how come—"

"Who did you tell?"

"Tell? What are you talking about? I don't know what you—"

"Wrong answer."

Bolan hated to terrorize a woman, but scaring this pretty kid into a confession was the only way he had of getting on target. He pushed her back against the gnarled bole of the tree and pressed his hand around her throat. "You played kiss-and-tell with someone after I left the hospital," he said. "Someone who must have picked me up at police headquarters when I was talking with Captain Fernandez, someone who tried to turn me into a red smear on the sidewalk. I want to know who."

"I'll say it again," the girl replied with a show of bravado. "I don't have any idea what you're talking about."

Bolan looked right and left. They were still alone in the park. "I've had a tough day," he said. "I'm tired. I get even more tired asking questions. I just might end our conversation, and the hospital'll have to look for a new receptionist."

She shook her head wordlessly.

Bolan exerted a small amount of pressure. She stiffened, mouth open in a silent scream. "I'll give you a five-count. It's up to you."

"I didn't tell anyone. Why would I?"

"One."

"I don't even know *why* you're interested. How could—"

"Two."

"Look, mister, I don't even know your name, but—"

"Three."

"For God's sake! How can I give you what doesn't exist?"

"Four."

"You got it all wrong!" the girl shouted. "There's nothing!"

"Five." Bolan flexed the muscles of his forearm and suddenly the girl broke.

"All right, all *right*," she sobbed. "You don't have to...I mean if you must know, I told Diego."

"Diego who?"

"Diego Olivera."

"Your boyfriend?"

The receptionist's dark eyes flashed. "Certainly not! I wouldn't be seen dead with trash like that!" She tossed her head defiantly.

"Then why?"

"He has...he has a hold on my family. My father borrowed money, and when he couldn't pay it back, they sent Diego to...to..." She was openly crying now, the tears streaming down her face.

Bolan stepped back. "Tell me about it," he said gently.

She looked up, surprised, and began to talk. The words tumbled out in a flood. Her father was a miner. He had been employed in the Caliente district until the coal seams narrowed so much that the workings, bored laterally into the mountainside, could only be operated by child labor. Out of work, he had gambled, lost, gambled again and then gone to the moneylenders in a vain attempt to recoup his losses and pay off his debts.

Then the sharks moved in.

The girl was the only member of the family who was working. Most of her income was forfeit, paying off the huge sums of compound interest that had accrued. In addition, on pain of foreclosure or legal action, she was forced to act as a spy or informer for the collector, Diego, anytime he wanted her to.

"And run occasional errands?" Bolan asked. "Such as delivering a small package to an uptown hotel or an envelope stuffed with bills to a policeman's home? That kind of thing?"

She nodded.

It was a familiar story, one that had touched a raw nerve. Mafia loan sharks had destroyed the Executioner's own family. His father, in the same position as the girl's, had discovered that Bolan's sister had become a prostitute to help pay off the interest—and, in a frenzy of grief and shame, he had shot dead his wife and daughter, wounded his younger son then killed himself. Deeply affected by the shattering experience, Mack Bolan had devoted his life to the eradication of those predators too smart or too ruthless to be caught within the net of the law.

And here was a chance to pay off one more installment of *his* debt to animal man.

"What's your name?" he asked the girl.

"Martina."

"And the family name?"

"Joaquim."

"Listen, Martina, as of tonight, you pay no more money, you take no more orders. The debt is canceled. Understand?"

Martina shook her head, brushing the back of one hand across her face where tears had channeled through the makeup. "I don't understand. Who are you? Why should you—"

"I'm no attorney from New York. Let's leave it at that. I'm sorry I had to act tough with you, but there was no other way. Now go home and stop worrying. Everything's going to be okay. Right now I need two addresses, yours and Diego's. The rest you can leave to me."

She jotted down the street numbers on the back of an envelope. Lines of tension around her mouth and eyes had noticeably slackened. The certainty in his voice imbued her with a sudden and unexpected confidence. Was this really someone who cared enough to help at last? Her lips twitched into the beginning of a smile. She started to speak, but the Executioner had vanished into the shadows.

3

The building was a rundown two-story frame house at the end of a dead-end street in a suburb east of the city. It was set among a stand of acacia trees on half an acre of wild grass strewn with discarded food containers and dozens of empty cans. The other homes that bordered the unpaved road were in better shape, but sagging porch timbers, weed-grown driveways and rusted sedans jacked up on bricks hinted that life, too, was a dead-end affair for many of their owners.

Clearly the development had been the brainchild of some property maven who had misjudged city folks' liking for steep hillsides and then stolen away, leaving half-completed streets and vacant lots to expire quietly under the onslaught of Mother Nature.

Bolan drove halfway down the road then continued the rest of the way on foot. Fading before he reached the gate into a clump of willow that drooped over the cracked sidewalk, he hoisted himself over the wall and dropped into waist-high weeds on the other side. Beyond the house, the serrated crest of the Cordillera gnawed at the star-spangled sky.

The warrior circled warily, avoiding piles of garbage and garden tools disintegrating among the invading grass. No lights showed at street level, but horizontal strips of yellow gleamed between the slats of shutters masking an upstairs window. The screen door of the back porch was unfastened. Bolan closed one gloved hand over the latch and eased it open.

A cord strung with empty cans and several cowbells was looped across the porch as a kind of primitive burglar alarm. Bolan ducked beneath it and approached the inner door. A bunch of slender steel implements dangled from his wrist.

Three minutes later there was a loud click and the door swung open.

He stiffened, right hand hovering over the Desert Eagle holstered at his hip, but there was no reaction from the dark interior. Faintly now he could hear the strains of rock music from the upper floor. He stood, padded into the room and switched on a penlight.

The thin beam revealed a ramshackle kitchen with a sink full of dirty dishes, a single mug half full of cold coffee among the bread crumbs dotting a plastic tabletop. Through an open doorway, he could see a passage that led past stairs to the front entrance.

He catfooted to the staircase. The rooms on either side of the hallway were dark and empty. The music, louder now, drowned out any noise he made creeping up the stairs, treading carefully at the side of each step to minimize creaks.

Light showed beneath a door facing the landing. Bolan put together the music, the lack of voices, the single coffee cup in the kitchen and came up with one as the number of inhabitants in the house.

Hefting the Desert Eagle in his right hand, he drew back a pace, lunged forward with his heel and kicked the door open.

Bright light momentarily dazzled him.

Beneath the unshaded bulb, small transparent envelopes lay scattered over a table with a scrubbed wood top. Nearby was a square plastic container holding about two pounds of white powder, a yellow measuring spoon and a bag of baker's flour. The man crouched over a bench in the shuttered window bay wore an expensive designer suit and two-tone pointy shoes. The hair curling behind his ears was dark and unkempt. Long sideburns and a slim mustache slashed the sallow skin of his face.

He whirled around as the door crashed open, one hand snatching at a 9 mm pistol on the bench.

"I wouldn't!" Bolan growled.

"Who are you? What the hell are you doing here?" The voice was high-pitched, the words dripping with venom.

"Who I am is of no importance. It's who you are that counts. Diego Olivera, right?"

"So?"

"Cutting the merchandise," Bolan said, nodding at the cluttered table, "to double the profits. Nice work for a small-timer."

"So you got the drop. So fucking what? Lay down the cards, man, or get lost."

"I'm here to settle an account. A final settlement. The name of the client is Joaquim."

"What do you mean settle? They owe—"

"They owe you nothing," the Executioner snapped. "I told you, the account is closed, as of tonight."

"Oh, yeah? I don't see a sack of bread in your hand."

"There's no money involved," Bolan replied. "Just the release you're going to sign. But before that you're going to tell me who your immediate boss is, why he's hot for news of the American couple injured in the car accident in the mountains, who killed them and why.''

''Man's crazy,'' Olivera sneered, talking to the ceiling. ''Out of his skull. He doesn't know what he's sayin'!''

Bolan had shifted the Desert Eagle to his left hand, the yawning .44-caliber muzzle lined up directly with the drug dealer's chest. He'd been watching the guy ease himself almost imperceptibly into a position where the pistol on the bench was within reach of his right hand. The Executioner fired two shots in rapid succession at the bench, sending the gun skittering to the floor.

''Now we'll start talking for real,'' Bolan said. ''You first, because you have more to say. And remember my aim is good—that buckled toy on the floor should tell you that.''

''Shit, man, there's nothing to say.''

''Just answer the three questions.''

''Seems like I forgot them.''

''Question number one—the name of your boss.''

''I'm free-lance. I don't have a boss. Some jerk contacts me when there's a job to be done. Another drops me the bread when it's over. End of story.''

''Wrong answer.''

''I tell you—''

Bolan walked briskly forward and pressed the muzzle of the big .44 against Olivera's forehead. ''Talk,'' the Executioner repeated, ''or I'll punch a hole through your skull big enough to push this gun through.''

''There is no boss,'' the Colombian croaked. ''I mean, like no boss direct. It's the cartel. They use a cutout, he's the only one I ever see. Guy by the name of Ortiz, Raul Ortiz.''

''Where can I find him?''

"I don't know. I always find a note fixing a meet pushed under the door. But I know a bar downtown where he hangs out sometimes," Olivera added hastily, seeing Bolan's lips tighten. "A place called The Snowman's Rest."

"The owner has a sense of humor," Bolan said grimly. "All right, let's go to number two. Why was the cartel so interested in the Americans when they were hospitalized?"

"You tell me. I was ordered to lean on the Joaquim woman and pass on anything relating to the foreigners—questions, visits, that sort of thing."

"How did you pass it on? Through Ortiz? A drop?"

"I leave messages in the mailbox outside this dump," Olivera said sullenly.

"So you don't live here?"

"Me? In this hole? You've got to be joking!"

"Okay," Bolan said. "It's just a packaging and distribution center, a place where the stuff at the lower end of the sewer is processed, right?"

"If you want to put it like that."

"That's exactly how I want to put it. Why were they killed?"

"Word was that they knew too much. They were taken out to stop them from passing it along the line, I'd guess."

"Too much about what? What were they into themselves?"

"How the hell should I know?"

"But it was a cartel job, one way or another?"

"Your guess." Olivera winced. "Jeez, my head!"

"Who did the killing?"

The Colombian tried to shrug. "They got hit men on tap for any situation. Some guys'll do anything for money."

"Really? Well, you're going to do something free. For once. You're going to sit at that table and write exactly what I tell you, the way I tell it, on your loan company's letterhead. Got it?"

"Loud and clear."

"So let's take it from the top." Bolan planted an undamaged chair in front of the littered table. With his free hand he swept everything on top onto the floor. He kicked over the plastic container so that the contents spilled, and stamped them into the rug.

"Hey!" Olivera yelled, struggling to his feet. "You know what that stuff costs?"

"I know what it costs in terms of human life and suffering. You better get that paper and sit down before I start on a balance sheet."

Bright blue cursive script spread the legend Pacific and Caribbean Finance, Inc. across the top of the paper. Bolan didn't trouble to read the names of the directors printed at the foot of the page; he knew they would be straw men, paid to lend their names—and, ideally, an air of respectability—to a shady enterprise of which they knew nothing. He tossed a ballpoint in front of the dealer and dictated a quittance addressed to the Joaquim family—a blanket release acquitting them of any further payment in respect of any and all contracts existing between them and the finance company, accrued debts to be considered as settled in full as of that date.

Olivera sweat blood as he laboriously wrote down the legal phrases. "You know what they'll do to me when they hear of this?'' he choked. "Christ, they'll crucify me!''

"That seems to make biblical sense," the Executioner said. "Look for me among the crowd.''

"You can laugh, you bastard.''

"I'll certainly try. Right now you can sign that release and seal it in an envelope with the company logo on it.''

Bolan stowed the envelope in a neoprene pouch clipped to the belt of his blacksuit. He looked around the shabby room. He wanted to make sure that the helldust littering the floor couldn't be salvaged to make more profits for the human vampires growing fat on the weaknesses of man. There was a quart of tequila on a buffet at the far end of the room. He unscrewed the cap and emptied the contents over the sachets and the spilled cocaine. Then he scooped up a matchbox and set fire to a sheet of paper, dropping the flaming leaf on the sodden mess. In a few seconds the fiery liquor ignited. Tongues of blue fire licked the floor.

Diego Olivera uttered a scream of rage. He dived for the pistol Bolan had knocked off the bench, whipped up the damaged weapon and swung on the big man with a grimace of hatred contorting his features.

Bolan's finger tightened on the .44's trigger before the Colombian squeezed death from the automatic. The big slug cored the gunner's right shoulder, slamming him back against the wall. The damaged gun dropped to the floor.

Olivera was a mess. Blood oozed between the clenched fingers of the hand clutching his injured shoulder, staining his expensive Italian threads. His crazed eyes burned with deadly hostility.

The flaming mass in the center of the room had set fire to the remaining chair and one leg of the table; the acrid cordite fumes were swamped now in the odor of burning wood. Brown smoke dimmed the brightness of the unshaded lamp.

Bolan coughed, releathering the big .44. He kicked the dealer's pistol into the middle of the blazing drug consignment. And suddenly the rock music, which had been blaring from the radio ever since he burst into the room, was cut off as heat shriveled the plastic insulation on the cord and melted the wires.

There was no sound but the crackle of flames and the rasp of Olivera's tortured breath. Bolan strode to the door. "So long, Diego," he called. "Good luck with the guys in the cartel. They're going to want an explanation for what happened to their product."

Bolan hurried down the stairs and let himself out into the street.

Behind him, Olivera was trying vainly to beat out the flames. The thumping and cursing were punctuated by sharp reports as the remaining rounds in the automatic's magazine exploded.

The warrior got into the rental and started the engine. He turned the car around and headed back toward the city center. Fifteen minutes later he parked outside the Joaquim home and dropped the envelope containing the release into the mailbox.

4

The Snowman's Rest was an artsy tavern with an eye on the tourist trade. Rustic tables, chairs and benches stood in front of lurid murals representing the white-capped peaks of the high Andes. On the split-pine wall above the bottles in back of the bar, ancient agricultural tools competed for space with skis, crampons and other mountain gear.

Bolan wore a checkered lumberjack shirt and a pair of Levi's. He ordered a beer and sat down at an empty table to check out the regulars.

It was five o'clock in the afternoon. Heat still shimmered over the melted tar on the city sidewalks; above the high-rise office buildings in downtown Medellín, a flaming sun subsided westward toward the hundred-mile-distant Pacific.

Most of the patrons were neighborhood material, seasoned with a sprinkling of visitors—Germans garnished with guidebooks and binoculars, Japanese tourists festooned with cameras, Americans in jeans and T-shirts. Bolan waited until he had finished his beer before approaching the bar. "Hey, Mac," he said to the bartender, "Ortiz been in today?"

"Ortiz?"

"Raul Ortiz. You know, the guy with friends in the right places." Bolan had no physical description of the cutout to offer.

The barman picked up a glass and began to polish it. "Never heard of him." He put down the glass and moved away.

"Great," the Executioner said to nobody in particular. "The guy tells me to look him up at the Snowman anytime I'm in town. So I came by, and the bartender hasn't even heard of him."

The place was filling up. Waiters in mountain costume swooped between the tables, shouting orders. Burly locals shouldered through the press around the bar. "You looking for Raul?" a Spanish-accented voice inquired at Bolan's left.

He swung around, saw a short, bearded man with a barrel chest.

"You got it," the warrior replied.

"Maybe I could help." His square-tipped, callused fingers were wrapped around a shot glass of rye.

"I'd like to think so," Bolan told him. "Buy you a drink?"

"Why not? Life was designed for the reckless."

"Ortiz isn't coming in today?" Bolan asked when the barkeep had filled the order.

"He's in the parking lot in back," the bearded man said. "He has business to attend to, this time of day. I'll take you there, if you want."

"Suits me." Bolan drained his glass. The business would be pushing coke to high-school kids on their way home. He didn't miss the quick glance exchanged between his new friend and the guy behind the bar as they turned to leave.

He was expecting trouble. He knew that an open, undisguised attempt to locate a cartel runner would almost certainly stir up trouble—especially if the people who had booby-trapped his car were still keeping tabs on him, knew in fact just who was doing the stirring. But Ortiz was the only lead he had; if he didn't provoke the cartel to action, he could stick around for days, getting no place. And a gut reaction, another Bolan hunch, told him that positive action on his own part was urgent.

But, primed though he was, he wasn't tuned enough to the local scene to guess from which direction the trouble would come.

There was a stoop in front of the bar and beside it, an alleyway led to the crowded parking lot. Beyond the rows of close-packed sedans, convertibles and limos, a tall motor home stood just inside a gateway leading to a back street. Two kids lounged against one of the vehicle's front fenders; a third was stepping down from a doorway in back. "Over there," the man with the beard said. "Raul'll be happy to see a familiar face."

Bolan had opened the front of the lumberjack shirt to feel the comforting bulge of the holstered Beretta when the torrid evening erupted within mind-blowing force, and the graveled surface of the lot spun up to crash against his face. Two men who had appeared from between a couple of station wagons seized his legs and dragged him away.

The bearded man followed, tapping the blackjack against his palm. "I'm Ortiz," he said. "As you know me so well, maybe you'll confide in me and spring the secret—who the hell are you, and what are you into?"

Before Bolan could formulate a reply, tires crunched on gravel as a roadster crammed with kids drove in through the rear entrance. "Get him under cover, quick," Ortiz growled.

Rough hands lifted the warrior from the ground. A third man opened the rear door of one of the station wagons, and he was bundled inside. The engine roared, and the vehicle lurched toward the exit before the Executioner's groggy mind was ready to handle the situation.

He lay on the floor with three pairs of feet grinding into his spine, between the inward-facing rear seats. Ortiz sat beside the driver, twisted around to face the three hardmen. He held Bolan's Beretta in his two hands. "Nice piece," he said. "Customized. Special suppressor. Quick-draw rig. Very professional."

Bolan remained silent.

"Friends of mine are anxious to know why an American should be prowling around here upsetting people and shoving his nose into their business. We're taking you to a nice quiet place where you can take as long as you like answering their questions."

"Wrong questions," Bolan stated. "You're the wrong Ortiz, is all. The guy I was hoping to meet is tall, with a slim build and has no whiskers. *You* got *me* wrong too—I'm an attorney from New York, briefed by an organization called SAFE."

"Save that for the cops," Ortiz cut in harshly. "The few we haven't bought yet."

"I'm not interested in your marketing patterns," Bolan said from the gritty floor. "What I want to know is, why should you—"

"Shut up!" one of the hardmen snarled, kicking Bolan in the ribs. "*We* ask the questions, right?"

Bolan stayed quiet, allowing his eyes to take in any available information that might help.

From where he lay, with one cheek pressed to the floor, he could squint up at the windows on the near side of the road. Soon the office towers and city buildings gave way to lower, suburban facades that slipped past faster as the wagon increased speed. The distance between streetlights grew, then there was nothing but telephone wires and an occasional tree zipping across the evening sky.

The Executioner reviewed the options. The station wagon was a Volvo with a single, upward-lifting rear door. Once it was unlatched, hydraulic pistons would raise it automatically to full height. Most hatches of this kind had no inside handle, but the Volvo was custom-built: because the two bench seats faced each other, there were no normal rear doors. There had to be a means for the passengers in back to exit.

That was behind him. Ortiz, in front, had removed the Beretta's magazine and shaken the shells into the palm of his hand. The driver was busy keeping the speeding vehicle on the country road. The three hardmen, one behind him, the others on the near side, would certainly be armed—but encumbered for a second or two if faced with an unexpected situation and required to draw fast.

A second or two was all the Executioner needed.

The Volvo slowed, then rumbled over a bridge. From the noise, Bolan guessed it was a railroad bridge.

If the highway ran over a railroad, that usually meant it was on top of an embankment.

Worth a gamble?

Affirmative, Bolan thought. It was time for action, and the hell with the odds. He tensed his muscles.

Ortiz had begun to say something about the Beretta when the warrior exploded into movement.

He shot his arms above his head, then swept them upward and outward, catching all three hardmen behind the knee—not forceful enough to knock them from the seats, but enough to unbalance them temporarily. At the same time he drew up his own knees, raised the top half of his body and hurled himself into a back somersault.

He hit the rear door, and the handle at its base, as Ortiz dropped the components of the Beretta and reached for his own gun.

One of the hardmen, the one sitting on his own, had recovered enough to jerk a Browning automatic from his waistband and take aim. The other two were still scrabbling when the door swung up and Bolan dropped from sight.

The two guns roared in a single explosive blast, but he was already below the line of the bumper, and the slugs scoured chunks of macadam from the road.

Bolan hit hard ground at thirty-five miles per hour, came out of a shoulder roll and was catapulted over the side of an embankment. He plunged among bushes covering the slope, snapped branches and came to rest on his back at the foot of a wooden fence that enclosed a field of grazing horses.

The Volvo's brakes were still screaming. The wagon finally stopped seventy yards beyond the place where Bolan had dropped. Doors swung open, and Ortiz and his men ran along the lip of the embankment.

Bolan lay still; he had no place to go. If they climbed down the slope and started shooting, there was nothing he could do.

Ortiz was shouting orders. The Colombians spread out and were about to start down among the bushes when a second squeal of brakes revealed a new arrival.

A Mercedes sedan stopped twenty yards behind the Volvo, and the driver's door opened. A tall, thin man wearing a panama hat and a pale gray suit got out and rushed over to Ortiz. Bolan couldn't hear what he said, but they seemed to be arguing. Then Ortiz and the hardmen—their weapons now out of sight—returned to the Volvo, got in and drove away.

"It's safe to come up now." For a moment Bolan didn't move. The man in the gray suit was standing at the top of the embankment and, surprisingly, the warrior realized that he knew the guy. It was years since they'd run across each other, but he knew him.

Hillyard Mannering came from an "old money" Philadelphia family, and he had commanded a search-and-destroy penetration unit similar to Bolan's own during the final days of the Vietnam War. Mannering had been a West Pointer, Bolan a sergeant, but there had been a mutual respect between the two men.

Bolan recognized the guy at once. The upright carriage, the head carried slightly on one side, the quizzical smile and the level stare from those pale blue eyes remained unchanged by the years.

Mannering, on the other hand, wouldn't recognize the Executioner: two separate sessions of plastic surgery since he'd first started his personal war against the Mob had altered beyond the grasp of any casual acquaintance the features of the man once known as Sergeant Mercy.

Maybe that was just as well, Bolan thought as he clambered back up to the roadway. Knowing who the guy was, had been, he would himself stay anonymous until a few cards were down.

Mannering held out a hand to help Bolan over the top. "Bad company you were keeping there," he said.

"Those guys are involved in the drug trade. I know one of them by sight."

He made no comment on the fact that the men had been armed, and he asked no questions. The Executioner offered no answers.

Interesting, nevertheless.

"I imagine you need a ride back into town," Mannering said. "I'd gladly take you there—" he gestured toward the Mercedes "—but I have to go out to my place in the country for half an hour and talk to my steward. Spot of trouble with one of the horses."

The well-modulated tenor voice, the slightly anglicized choice of words, Bolan noted, had changed as little as the man's appearance.

"No problem," he replied. "I can hitch. I'm obliged for your intervention."

"On the other hand," Mannering said, "you could come out and sip a drink, if you've nothing better to do, and I'll run you back later. I have to be in the city soon after dark."

"Suits me." Bolan shrugged. He was intrigued. What was this ex-soldier doing in Colombia? Why had he so coolly assumed that Bolan must have been escaping from kidnappers? What had he said to Ortiz and his men? Why didn't he ask any questions? The Executioner reckoned it was worth an hour of his time to find out more.

After introductions, the Executioner settled in the passenger seat of the Mercedes, and the car purred away toward the mountains.

The "place" was located in a wooded valley fifteen miles from Medellín—thirty acres of green countryside enclosed by a white fence, with stables, paddocks and apple orchards tastefully arranged around a central, hacienda-style ranch house. Everything about the property, from the mosaic-tiled fountains in the courtyard to the rows of immaculate greenhouses in back, spelled money.

"Nice place."

"It's only rented," Mannering said apologetically. "I couldn't possibly afford to buy a place like this. The horses, actually, are only a kind of hobby. I don't sell them."

"Is that so? What business are you in?"

"Actually," Mannering replied, "it's not so much a business as a foundation. It was started by my old man—an organization known as SAFE—Save America from Evil."

"Really!" Bolan was surprised by the coincidence.

"You're heard of the foundation?" Mannering raised his eyebrows.

"Sure I have. In a way I'm in the country because of it," Bolan replied, maintaining his cover.

"You are?" Mannering brought the sedan to a halt, got out and handed the keys to a white-jacketed houseman who ran down the steps leading to the shingled adobe ranch house.

"I'm an attorney, and I told the police I'd been retained by SAFE," Bolan continued as they walked into a cool hallway. "That was because the people I was checking out had said *they* belonged—a couple of Americans who totaled an expensive roadster up in the mountains. But I guess you know about that."

"Of course. They were using our name as a cover, after all. But they had nothing to do with us." Mannering led the way into a book-lined library furnished with leather armchairs and glass-topped cabinets displaying pre-Colombian artifacts.

"That's what I was told," Bolan said. "Do you have any idea what these people *were* into?"

"Good Lord, yes. The man was an agent from some Washington security organization. He was following up a drug connection linking certain politicians in this country with a Florida syndicate. It seems he'd managed to infiltrate the Medellín cartel and was working for them undercover as a runner. The woman was a piece of window dressing to strengthen his flashy image."

"And they were killed to stop a report of whatever it was he'd found from reaching Washington?"

Mannering shrugged. "That's the way I'd read it."

"How would you read the car accident? Sabotage?"

Another shrug. "Sabotage? A staged blockage provoking an accident? Genuine mischance? Who knows? What we do know is that the drug barons were in there enough to take advantage. The guy was blown."

"That's clear enough," Bolan agreed. "Hell, I could have saved myself a lot of legwork if I'd known you knew that, if I'd known where to come."

"Yes," Mannering agreed. "If you'd known where to come."

"One thing I don't understand," Bolan went on. "Here you are with this property, but when the police started checking out the SAFE angle, they were told the organization had no representation in Colombia. The policeman I saw at the hospital—"

"Of course they were told that," Mannering interrupted. "Hell, cocaine's the country's biggest export! You have to go a long way and look damned hard before you find a family that doesn't have at least one member involved one way or another in the drug scene. The police are even worse. How much cooperation do you think we'd get if we openly set up a system designed to destroy the country's biggest foreign currency trade—and freeze out the biggest importer?''

"So you work entirely underground?"

"I have to. I'm a horse breeder, a crazy *yanqui* with more money than business sense, who spends a lot of time and wastes a lot of his dollars on a rented property halfway to the Andes foothills. The policeman you saw—a Captain Fernandez, wasn't it?—is a rare bird here—an honest, conscientious officer. But he's up against a wall a hundred feet high. Anyway, he'd be taken off the case at once if he stepped out of line. Or meet with an 'accident.'"

"I know what you mean," Bolan said.

"I thought you would, Counsellor," Mannering replied. He rang a bell and told the houseman, when he appeared, to bring a beer and sandwiches for his guest. "I have to go out to the stables now," he said, "but I'll be with you in less than a half hour."

When he had gone, the Executioner strolled to a window overlooking the driveway and the paddocks. Dusk had given way to darkness. A cloud bank rolling up from the mountains reflected the distant lights of the city beyond the somber bulk of trees standing sentinel on both sides of the entrance gates. Was he mistaken or had he glimpsed sentinels of a more mobile variety, hard-faced men with suspiciously bulging jackets, moving among those trees when they arrived?

Hillyard Mannering talked horses when he returned. They were halfway back to the city, approaching the embankment where Bolan had escaped from Ortiz and his men, before he stopped enthusing over brood mares and yearlings.

Then, when the railroad bridge materialized at the far end of the bright tunnel carved by the Mercedes's headlights, he shot Bolan a swift glance and said, "Belasko, I see you as a New York attorney about as easily as I see myself in the role of a revivalist preacher."

Bolan grinned. "So?"

"So whatever it was that you came here to find out went down the drain when this guy Sercondini was liquidated. They got him before he could pass it on. So, apart from that fact, you got nothing to report to whoever did brief you. So now, by my reckoning, you should be a man looking for a job. And you look like you can take care of yourself."

Mannering drove for a while in silence, then, "By chance I have need of such a person. It follows that I have a proposition to make."

"I'm listening."

"This is classified material, but I can tell you that, as well as acting as South American Director for SAFE, I'm also compiling a dossier of highly sensitive material for Interpol."

"Still listening."

"The brief was to collect the max of damning intel on—I quote—the vast and frightening international drug traffic and the crime it provokes. End of quote."

"And Colombia's as good a place as any to start."

"You could say that. My work here's almost completed, but there's a coke farm in the Cordillera that I still have to hit. After that I'm booked abroad a cruise liner, the *American Dream*, that leaves Barranquilla in a couple days' time."

"A cruise liner?"

"Can you think of a better cover? The ship's on a Caribbean run, stopping off in Venezuela, Haiti, Rio and the French West Indian island of Martinique. In all of which I can go ashore and check out the local underworld, effecting penetration if possible.''

"Sounds good," Bolan said noncommitally.

"Here's my proposition. Some of these shore forays are going to be kind of hairy, and I need someone to ride shotgun. I want a guy who can act as troubleshooter, bodyguard, hit man, whatever. But it has to be someone who can pass for a business connection or a golfing buddy or suchlike. Somebody who'll be accepted as my companion aboard ship, not a gorilla with biceps and and brain the size of a walnut. You read me?''

"All the way."

"Okay. My guess is that you and I are on the same wave length. Guess number two would be that, like me, you rate the drug scene as a target ripe for destruction. Am I right?''

"You got it."

Mannering nodded. "I'd like you to be this guy. On terms to be arranged. To be handled, practically, any way that suits you.''

"I'm not a mercenary," Bolan said. "I'm not for hire, but I'm heavily into any activity that's on the antidrug agenda. I might be prepared to try this on for size. On one condition.''

"Name it."

"I'd like to spend one day backtracking on the couple killed in the hospital. Just in case there could be a handle someplace along the route they traveled, something Fernandez and his men missed. Allow me time for that, and you're on.''

Mannering removed a hand from the steering wheel and held it out. "Twenty-four hours.''

BOLAN FOUND THE SITE of the wreck without any problem. Reports filed in the newspaper morgue guided him to the right section of highway, and once he reached it the evidence was plain enough. The brushwood on the hillside was still scarred and flattened where the salvage cranes had penetrated to drag away the remains of the Maserati. Above, a trail of earth, rock and shattered stone fanned out from the breached wall of the country road that curved up around the flank of the mountain.

Bolan left the highway and parked the rental fifty yards below the fatal hairpin. He walked up and across to the damaged parapet. There wasn't much to see: the gap in the stonework; the remains of chalk marks made by police investigators on the scorching macadam; nearer the curve, where the mountain scrub shimmered in the heat haze rising from the road, four black skid marks angled across the surface.

Clearly—if the marks were indeed made by the Maserati—the roadster had been out of alignment, drifting partially sideways when the driver braked. He must, Bolan reckoned, have taken the corner too fast, seen the truck, jammed on the brakes when he had already lost the back end, then released them and tried to get through.

Strolling around the bend, the warrior crouched down until his head was about level with the eyeline of a sports car driver. As he had thought, the road beyond the hairpin was hidden by the rock shoulder.

There wasn't much traffic. An ancient bus full of Indian women wearing black derbies over bright head scarves rattled down toward the highway in first gear; a silver Stingray hissed past on its way up into the Cordillera. Bolan walked slowly back to the SEAT, fanning his face with a newspaper. An old man with a wide-brimmed straw hat and a blanket over one shoulder had halted his mule beside the car. The Executioner greeted him politely in Spanish.

"A good day to you," the old man replied. "And a good route." He looked at the sky. No clouds were visible. "It is indeed a good day for those who travel prudently. But no day is good for those who would arrive before their time. I see that you are investigating the signs that prove haste leads only to disaster."

"You saw the accident?"

"Naturally. I am always on the road at this time."

"But you didn't come forward in answer to the police radio appeal."

"You will forgive me, but are you with the police? The American police?"

"No, no. My name is Belasko, and I'm a lawyer."

"So. A lawyer. Rafael Mendoza at your service," the old man said courteously, holding out a seamed hand. "As to the police, when you attain my age you learn that it is wise to avoid unnecessary contact with them. I have seen many different police forces, and today's friend may be tomorrow's enemy. Also," he added, "I do not possess a radio."

"But you did see the accident," Bolan probed, shaking the hand. "Why do you think it happened?"

"They were driving too fast. There was a truck. But then they always went too fast. Man is not intended for such speeds."

"Always? You had seen the couple before?" Bolan asked.

"I had seen them a number of times," Rafael Mendoza was saying. "Perhaps once a week, perhaps twice.

It could not be more frequently because they live so far away.''

''You know where they came from?''

''Yes. From far, from very far away. As I have said.''

''Do you know the name of the place?''

''That I cannot tell you. But it was beyond the first of the cordilleras, in a distant place where men dig fuel from the mountains.''

''In a mining area? But how can you possibly know this?''

''Simply,'' the old man said. He extended an arm toward the tree-covered crests thrusting into the burnished sky. On the road somewhere above, an automobile windshield flashed in the sun. ''Below the pass, Pedro Díaz keeps a small shack where he sells refreshing drinks and trinkets for tourists who stop to admire the view. Each afternoon I pause to bid him a good day and drink a little wine with him. He knows— he knew—the couple well. They stopped there often, and sometimes they would make a telephone call. I myself heard the man do this once.''

''You heard what he said? Do you remember the town he called?''

''I cannot recall the name, but Pedro said it was a small place, beyond the region where they dig the fuel.''

''One final question. If you could see both the car *and* the truck, you must have been farther up the hillside. Did you see anything else, anything at all, that might have had something to do with the accident? Was there anyone else around?''

Mendoza shook his head. ''Not at the time of the accident, no.'' He indicated the empty panniers slung each side of the mule. ''As you see, I bring fruit and vegetables down to the market each morning. I remember the truck was already there when I returned. I saw a car drive away as I rounded the corner. I thought perhaps the driver had been talking to the trucker, and I remember wondering why the man had chosen to wait there, where the sun is hot and there is no shade. But no, when I looked back later and he was turning the truck, there was no one else.''

He was waiting for Harvey Lee. It had been a setup.

"You have been most helpful. Thank you.''

"It is nothing.''

Bolan got behind the wheel of the rental, turned it around and drove back down the mountain road toward the highway and the city.

"God go with you," the old man called as he mounted the mule and urged the beast to continue its laborious ascent.

Higher up the hill, the driver of the silver Corvette put away his field glasses and opened the vehicle's trunk. He propped up the lid of a small shortwave transmitter-receiver and maneuvered its switches and dials. Then he held a single headphone to one ear and spoke quietly into a hand mike.

"Ortiz," he announced. "Belasko quit the hotel early and drove to the place where we took out the Maserati. He spent fifteen minutes poking around and talking to some peasant with a mule. It seemed the peasant was handing him a story. Now he's on his way back to town. He saw me pass, so you better tell Rodrigo to pick him up at the intersection below. Yeah, still the red SEAT. How's that? Oh, sure. No sweat. I'll take care of it right away.''

He backed up the car and coasted down the grade. After the third curve, he saw Rafael Mendoza jogging slowly toward him on his mule.

Ortiz steered a few yards past him and braked. He got out of the car and called, "Hey, you! Old man!"

The mule continued on, Mendoza not bothering to turn his head.

Cursing, Ortiz dropped his cigarette to the ground, swiveled his heel on the butt and shouted again. "You! Peasant! Are you deaf?"

This time Mendoza turned his head and spoke without checking the pace of the mule. "Are you addressing me?"

"Of course I'm addressing you, you old fool," Ortiz snapped. "Do you see any other peasants on this son of a bitch road?"

The old man reined in the mule and waited patiently while Ortiz strode up to him. "What do you want with me?" he asked.

"First, I want to teach you to speak when you're spoken to, peasant. Get off that mule."

Mendoza sat silent and regarded him impassively.

"I said get off!" Ortiz roared. He raised his right forearm and backhanded the old man viciously across the face. Mendoza's broad-brimmed hat fell to the ground, and his leathery cheek flushed a dull red with the blow. Yet still he stared unflinchingly at his aggressor.

Ortiz hit him again, a wicked right to the solar plexus. The old man gave a choking grunt, folded forward over the neck of the mule and slid to the road.

The drug dealer drew back his foot. He was wearing tan-and-white shoes with pointed toe caps. He kicked Mendoza three times, once on the side of the head and twice in the kidneys. After a while the old man rolled slowly over and tried to sit up, supporting himself on gnarled hands. He spit blood into the dust.

"Why...why do you do this...to me?" he croaked. A thin thread of scarlet ran from one side of his bruised mouth.

Ortiz made no reply. Measuring his distance carefully, he drew back his foot for the fourth time and he caught the old man full on the chin. This time Mendoza didn't get up.

The rasp of a cicada in a tree across the road shivered into silence as Ortiz straightened his necktie, smoothed down the front of his cream shantung suit and looked around cautiously. The stretch of road between the curves lay empty in the sun. Neither humans nor vehicles were visible among the wooded undulations massed against the hot blue sky. The mule stood motionless in a patch of shade cast by a stunted oak, its head hanging low.

Ortiz seized the unconscious figure of Rafael Mendoza by the shoulders and dragged it into the road not far from the spots of blood already congealing darkly in the dust.

After a final look around, he combed his fingers through his beard, lighted a cigarette and walked quickly back to his vehicle.

He backed the car a hundred yards up the grade. Then, steering with care, he gunned the engine and accelerated toward the body sprawled on the blacktop.

5

Bolan heard the siren of the second ambulance when he was still two miles from the pass. It was some way behind him but climbing fast. When he saw the flashing blue light in his driving mirror, he pulled his vehicle to one side of the mountain road and waved the driver past.

There'd been no siren screaming when he passed the first one; it had been rolling sedately downhill toward the highway, not far from the place where Harvey Lee's Maserati had left the road.

Bolan didn't connect the two until he reached the Díaz shack, strategically placed at one side of the saddle. The second ambulance, its blue light still revolving, stood at the center of a group of men at the roadside. Beyond it was an amber light, on the roof of a Chevrolet patrol car. Bolan recognized the lean figure of Captain Fernandez among the white-coated medics and passersby. He parked beside two sedans and a dilapidated pickup and went to join him.

The policeman recognized the warrior and nodded. "If you wanted to talk to Díaz," he said, "you're too late. He died before we arrived."

"What happened?"

Fernandez shrugged. "Some kind of personal quarrel perhaps. The place is all smashed up inside." He smiled, but there was no humor in the grimace. "So was Díaz. He'd been badly beaten, then whoever did it switched to a hammer. He was still breathing when the ambulance arrived . . . just. But we were too late."

"Did he say anything?"

"No."

"I was going to meet someone here," Bolan stated. "An old guy with a mule, name of Mendoza. I didn't see him on the road."

"He was killed by a hit-and-run driver a half hour before this happened."

"Mendoza and Díaz were buddies," Bolan said thoughtfully. "The old man actually witnessed the accident down below. According to him, the truck that caused the crash was a plant." He stared out beyond the groundswell of wooded ridges, out to the last crest, where the bare, serrated peaks of the Andes shimmered in the heat. "Also according to him, Díaz knew the American couple, knew that they stayed somewhere back in those hills. Do you, like me, find just a hint of a connection there?"

Fernandez sighed. "I'll follow it up and make all the moves. But you know where it'll lead me."

Bolan knew. He'd have known even if Hillyard Mannering hadn't told him. He'd been around long enough to know how bad the corruption really was.

He said goodbye and headed back to the city. He had to hand it to the cartel—its people were smart and they were efficient. Because of them, he'd gotten exactly nowhere.

Back in his hotel, Bolan picked up a copy of the local daily newspaper and read a short item on the front page.

The bullet-riddled body of Diego Olivera, 38, a convicted vice racketeer and suspected drug trafficker, was found early today on a vacant lot in the western suburbs of the city. Olivera, who had been shot eight times in the back with an automatic weapon, was thought to be a victim of gangland vengeance. One factor puzzling police investigating the killing, however, was a ninth wound, caused by a bullet of a different caliber, which had fired from in front. "The possibility that Olivera had in some way incurred the enmity of two rival factions in the underworld cannot be ruled out," a homicide squad spokesman told this reporter.

"You got that right," the Executioner murmured as he laid down the newspaper. The longer the law thought that, the more time it would take them to tumble to the fact that the dealer was executed because he was careless with several million dollars' worth of narcotics.

THE COKE FARM in the Cordillera that the SAFE director had to hit turned out to be the scene of an exploit that was tougher—and more literal—then Mack Bolan had been led to expect.

At the ranch house, Mannering led the Executioner into a gun room and opened a locked, glass-fronted cabinet and took out a Walther MP-K submachine gun. The cabinet also held a rack of single- and double-barreled sporting guns, a Skorpion machine pistol, several automatics and a Salvinelli .458-caliber competition rifle with a Winchester lever action. "That's quite a collection you got there," Bolan said.

Mannering smiled. "It's kind of a hobby. This really is the prize piece." He indicated the twin-barrel Salvinelli, with chased-silver butt plates. "I have to have a special insurance policy for it."

"At what that must have cost, I'm not surprised," Bolan said. "Are you using the MP-K tonight?"

"Plus a Combat Master. We may need firepower. Are you carrying?"

"Desert Eagle," Bolan said briefly. "I had a Beretta in a quick-draw rig, but Ortiz took it. I need something light and fast. What do you have?"

"No Berettas," Mannering said, "but I can give you a Colt Delta Elite." He reached into the cabinet.

While Bolan was adjusting a shoulder holster that his host passed over, Mannering loaded a 32-round box magazine with 9 mm shells and slammed it into the feeder housing in front of the Walther's trigger guard. "You want a tryout with that Colt before we leave?" he asked.

Bolan shook his head. "Rides good," he said, leathering the pistol. "Smooth action. Good balance. Very nice."

Mannering locked the cabinet. "Okay. We're on our way."

They drove a tall, square-cut Toyota Land Cruiser. A great deal of the two-hour journey was in first gear, as the sturdy 4 x 4 labored up the steep grades or maneuvered around unfenced, precipitous curves on the mountain roads penetrating the Cordillera.

Mannering parked the Toyota behind a jumble of huge boulders at the far end of a gulch saddling the fourth or fifth ridge they climbed, and they continued the journey on foot. The gulch opened out into an upland plain that sloped gently north and east. There were buildings half a mile away, but the land as far as the eye could see was planted with a crop that swayed blackly in the night as a breeze rustled down the pass. "Erythoxylum," Mannering murmured. "Cocaine itself is an alkaloid, but this is the stuff it comes from."

This was no news to the Executioner, but he grunted an acknowledgment. "You said we were hitting this place," he said. "So what's the deal? Are we here to teach someone a lesson? To choke off the grower?"

"We're destroyers," Mannering said simply.

The dirt road arrowing between the fields toward the buildings glimmered palely through the dark. The plain was five thousand feet above sea level, and the air settling down from the jagged peaks surrounding it was cold. Bolan turned up the collar of his jacket as they strode in single file through the grasses at the edge of the road.

No light showed from the buildings. As they approached, the warrior saw a central building two stories high, flanked by a line of low, flat-roofed outbuildings. When they were two hundred yards from the nearest one, dogs started to bark.

Half a minute later they heard the patter of feet on the road. "I'll handle this," Mannering said in a low voice.

Bolan said nothing. He eased the Desert Eagle from its holster, pulled back the slide and thumbed the safety. The dogs were very near, growling softly in their throats. He was aware of a moving blur against the pale ribbon of road, then a brilliant ray of light lanced out from beside him. He saw that there were two of them—huge Dobermans with red-flecked eyes. For an instant they halted, dazzled by the beam, black lips writhed back to expose inch-long fangs. Then Mannering shifted the flashlight to illuminate two hunks of raw meat he'd taken from a canvas sack clipped to his waist and thrown into the road.

The dogs lowered their heads, snuffling. "Stay absolutely still," Mannering whispered. Bolan had already frozen, the big gun rock-steady in his right hand.

The Dobermans worried the meat, holding the lumps down with one paw and tearing at the bloody flesh and fibers. Before they chomped down the last shreds, their front legs were buckling. Finally both keeled over and lay still. "The stuff in there will keep them quiet for an hour," Mannering muttered. "Come on. Let's go."

They set off at a trot. Bolan was feeling somewhat uneasy. It was a long time since he'd played second fiddle to anyone, and the role didn't sit well. Normally he did his own recon, made the assault plans. On this particular hit he had no specific briefing, nor did he know the long-term effect of what he was doing. He knew that he was helping someone fight the drug trade. That was good enough for this one operation, but on the upcoming cruise, he resolved, he was either one hundred percent in on the concept and planning, or it was no dice. Riding shotgun was one thing; acting as hired, unpaid help was another. As far as the Executioner was concerned, that was strictly a no-go situation.

Mannering had slowed. Now he crouched among the grass. Ahead in the distance they could hear voices.

"Fucking dogs," someone said in a surly tone. "Supposed to be well trained, and they just disappear into the night and—"

"Come on! They probably homed on some food with legs—a gopher, a prairie dog, something like that."

"The dogs took off, I tell you. They were barking. They heard something."

"I'm tellin' you. They're out chasing some critter."

"I saw a light."

"What you mean, a light?"

"For God's sake, Frank. A light. Like a car headlight or something."

Frank let loose a theatrical sigh. "You see many cars passing along this road tonight? Maybe it was the midnight bus on the way to Bogotá?"

"Go on, laugh. The dogs were after something. Why don't we hear them anymore?"

"Shit," Frank said, "we don't hear them because whatever it was, they found it and they're eating it!"

Mannering was flat on his face, worming his way through the grass. The two guards were about twenty yards ahead. Evaluating the sounds of the voices as they came to him, Bolan reckoned the men were just inside a gateway in a split-cane fence surrounding a yard in front of the nearest outbuilding.

"For God's sake," Frank went on, "if it bugs you, let's call the fuckers and you'll see. Hey! Pedro! Rex! Pedro—come on!"

There was silence, except for a faint moan of wind, a rustle of grass.

Frank called a second time. "You see," the other man said accusingly when there was still no response, "there's something here that smells. You better go around the back and ask Brett if he hears anything."

Bolan heard a muttered curse, then the sound of receding footsteps.

Mannering was on his feet and running. Bolan tried to restrain him, but he was too late. The guy was on top of the remaining sentry before the Executioner had risen upright.

The sentry whirled as Mannering leaped. The two fell to the ground, and there was an instant of confused struggling, then a choking gurgle. The struggles subsided. Bolan was familiar with the noise: he knew that Mannering had used a knife. But telegraphing his approach in that way allowed the sentry to yell a warning. And half a second before the sentry died, the report of a heavy-caliber revolver had momentarily limned the adversaries in a livid muzzle-flash.

Bolan cursed softly. Mannering was courageous enough, but foolhardy and inexperienced. Any chance they had of a surprise attack was gone. Lights had sprung on behind the shutters at several windows in the main building. Someone was shouting orders.

The warrior heard the pounding of feet as the sentry who'd run off returned to his post. He shifted the Colt from its shoulder rig and nestled the pistol grip in the palm of his left hand. The Desert Eagle already filled his right. He sprinted toward the gateway.

Mannering had briefed him on the general layout of the place when they parked the Toyota, and outlined the zones of attack each man would concentrate on. "There'll be ten or twelve of them," he had said. "And we have to take them all out before we can get on with the real work."

Bolan followed him into the yard, then cast himself down behind a cultivating machine with fat ribbed tires. A Jeep was parked beyond it, and Mannering was already prone beneath the rear wheels. Flame stabbed the night as his Walther submachine gun erupted in a short lethal burst that cut down the running sentry, for an instant silhouetted against a rectangle of yellow light.

The light vanished as someone slammed the door that allowed it to escape. But Bolan had time to track the Desert Eagle on two fleeting shapes that had raced into the yard.

The .44 Magnum belched fire three times, the awesome blast of its delivery echoing thunderously. The range was maximum for accurate targeting, around two hundred yards, but one of the shots scored—a body slammed against the wall of the house, fell and lay still. A high-pitched screech of pain followed by stumbling footsteps indicated that one of the other rounds had at least winged a defender.

Mannering's Walther ripped off another burst, which was succeeded by several single shots from his Combat Master automatic. But by now the defenders were getting it together. Automatic gunfire hosed toward them from all directions. Bolan had rolled into the open. The Desert Eagle's impressive muzzle-flash all too easily revealed his position. Slugs thumped into the cultivator's tires and bodywork then caromed skyward.

Bolan raised the Colt and pumped 10 mm zingers at the muzzle-flashes. One of the gunners yelled in pain; another shouted curses. Close at hand a calm voice was rapping out orders, coordinating fire from the gunners outside and those shooting from the darkened second-floor windows.

Bolan decided to put into action the next phase of the plan he had agreed with the SAFE director. If they waited until the enemy established definitive defense positions, the assault would become far more hazardous. "I'm making it now," he called to Mannering. "Cover me."

Over to his left, a fresh 32-pound box magazine clacked into place beneath the Walther's feeder housing. Jagged tongues of fire spit from under the Jeep as Mannering hammered short bursts across the facade and upper windows of the house. Glass shattered and crashed to the ground. One gunner dropped his weapon and plummeted from a window. Bolan scrambled to his feet and ran.

He covered ten yards, fifteen, dropped to the ground and emptied the Colt magazine, then dashed again, crouched low, for the corner of the low building. He made it inches ahead of a hail of bullets that scuffed the ground at his feet and chipped away fragments of the adobe wall, which stung his cheek.

As Mannering had said, there was a stack pipe against the wall. Bolan holstered both guns and began to climb. He was almost level with the flat roof when stars above the parapet blacked out and the head and shoulders of a man appeared in silhouette. The dark shape straightened, and Bolan saw the outline of an arm, a hand and a gun.

He acted automatically. There was no time to reach his own weapons. Years of urban guerrilla experience kicked in the instinctive reflex that powered the only possible reaction.

Bolan let go of the pipe and reached up in a single swift movement, grabbing the guy's shirtfront in both hands as he allowed himself to fall backward into space. They hit the ground fifteen feet below at the same time, with an impact that knocked the breath from their bodies. Because he was expecting it, the Executioner recovered first. He rolled on top of the man, jamming an elbow into his throat. He seized one flailing arm and smashed the back of the gunhand against the wall so that the weapon spun from his adversary's savaged fingers. Then he eluded a punch to the head and sprang to his feet.

Bolan feinted a kick to the groin. As the gunner's jerked up in spontaneous reaction, he leaned in and rammed the edge of his outstretched hand into the guy's throat.

The gunner folded and hit the dust.

Bolan reached once more for the stack pipe.

The flat roof stretched away toward the house. He catfooted to the edge and lay prone. There had been a lull in the firing. Mannering had moved—part of their plan was to conceal the fact that there were only two of them—but now he opened up again with the Combat Master. The deep-throated .45 autoloader choked out a succession of single shots while Bolan shoved another clip into the Colt.

He transferred the Desert Eagle to his left hand and sighted the smaller gun on a sector of the yard that lay between the main door of the house to the gateway and the machine that had been his original cover. Most of the defenders seemed to be concentrated there, behind a stack of lumber, around what looked like a flatbed trailer. When muzzle-flashes winked to one side of the lumber, he squeezed a pair of 10 mm flesh-shredders at the dark shape behind the flickering points of light.

The muzzle-flashes canted abruptly skyward. Bolan heard a stifled cry, a stumbling clatter as the shooter fell. He ducked behind the parapet—the sharp reports of the Colt's wildcat-size round had been lost in the sharp stammer of autofire, and the gunners below had their backs turned to his muzzle-flashes.

Mannering was behind a row of oil drums on the far side of the yard. The flashlight beam lanced suddenly toward the house, casting a fan of subdued illumination on each side of the brilliant central ray and revealing figures sheltered by the trailer and the lumber.

Bolan downed three of them with successive shots before a fourth man whirled around to pump a hail of lead roofward, showering the Executioner with stone fragments as he dropped from sight. The gunner didn't live long enough to go for broke. Steel-jacketed slugs from the Walther lashed across his back and cut him almost in two. A second later, Mannering blew away a marksman who had just shot out the flashlight, which had been wedged between two drums.

Bolan realized silence had fallen over the yard.

"There are one or two on the upper floor, then that's it," Mannering called.

Bolan, still lying facedown behind the parapet, was about to reply when a slight sound above and behind alerted him to danger. He flashed a glance over his right shoulder and made out the indistinct but menacing snout of a short-barreled automatic weapon aimed toward the voice in the yard.

The warrior had only a second to act. He dropped the Colt, rolled onto his back, raised both arms above his head and fired the Desert Eagle two-handed.

The gunner on the roof slammed against the chimney, slid scrabbling down the slope of shingles and dropped with a wild cry to the ground.

"I'm going in!" Mannering yelled. Bolan heard twin detonations and a splintering crash as his companion shot out the lock and kicked in the door below.

"I'm with you one floor up!" the Executioner called.

He stood and ran to the edge of the flat-roofed outbuilding. There was a gap of three or four feet between the structure and the wall of the house. Just above the level of the flat roof, an arched window frame supporting a single sheet of glass was set in the wall. Bolan reckoned it was at the end of an upper hallway.

He backed off a few yards, flexed his muscles, then sprinted forward. Taking off from the parapet, he launched himself across the gap and dived, arms crossed over his face, at the window.

The glass burst inward, and a fountain of razor-sharp fragments lacerated his forearms as he hurled through, shoulder-rolled and came up in a combat crouch.

The dark hallway was empty. At the far end, a thread of wavering light indicated a room illuminated by candles or an oil lamp. He heard voices, but they sounded far away.

The voices were drowned by an earsplitting explosion from somewhere below. Mannering had used one of the grenades that Bolan knew he carried in the canvas sack.

Confused shouting was followed by a fusillade of revolver shots, which were in turn eclipsed by the rasping clamor of the Walther submachine gun. There was a reaction, too, from the room at the end of the hallway. Someone cursed, a piece of furniture was moved and feet scraped on wooden floorboards.

Bolan raced forward, shouldered open the door and burst into the room.

Two men were in the room—a beefy South American fisting a heavy six-chambered revolver, and a smaller European with a mini-Uzi. They had been dragging a massive refectory table forward with the intention of blocking the door.

Shaken by the Executioner's eruption into the room, the South American had time to blast off only one thunderous shot that splintered the door frame beside the warrior's head. Bolan fired a quick shot that drilled him through the heart. Then he turned his attention to the guy with the mini-Uzi. A lethal stream of 10 mm slugs hammered into his body half a second before he could bring up the deadly subcompact and fire.

Flung backward by the multiple impacts, blood spurting from the ruin of his chest, the gunner cannoned into a side table carrying an oil lamp. The table collapsed, the dead man thumped to the floor, the lamp teetered and fell.

The glass shattered and kerosene spilled from the ruptured reservoir. Flame from the still-burning wick ignited the volatile liquid. In a moment the floor was ablaze, and flames were licking at the legs of the side table. Bolan got out of there and made the stairway.

"You score up there?" Mannering's voice floated up the well.

"Five on five," Bolan replied. "All quiet on your front?"

"That's affirmative."

The Executioner went down below. Light from another oil lamp spread slowly over the first floor as he crossed the entrance lobby. Mannering was standing amid a desolation of matchwood, broken glass and fallen plaster.

"Now we can start tonight's serious business," Mannering stated.

He holstered his Combat Master and slung the submachine gun over one shoulder.

Smoke poured down the stairwell and rolled across the yard as they emerged into the open air. Clouds of it, teased away by the night wind, boiled from the window Bolan had dived through, flickering redly with reflections from the fire inside.

"A good blaze will help," Mannering observed, "but we'll have to fire up our own if the job's to be done properly."

He led the way to the outbuildings that flanked the house. Fertilizer sacks, wicker-covered carboys, drums of chemical and farming machinery covered the floor space of the one on the left. The right-hand structure was the one Bolan had climbed. A gasoline-operated generator thumped beneath the roof of a lean-to in back of the building. The power fueled an air-conditioning plant that kept the interior at a cool, dry, even temperature.

Three aisles split the length of the store. Slatted wooden shelves, ceiling-high, were packed with hundreds of kilo packs of cocaine, culled from the fields that stretched away as far as the eye could see.

"In a couple of weeks' time," Mannering said, "that stuff, extracted, refined, packaged and cut, would have been on sale on the streets of New York, Chicago and San Francisco. We're here to stop it."

Half a dozen forty-gallon drums of gasoline were ranged beside the generator housing. They rolled two of them inside the store and knocked out the bungs, allowing the flammable liquid to gurgle out and spread over the floor. With smarting eyes and constricted throats, Bolan and the SAFE director ran clear of the sweetish aromatic stench and breathed in the fresh air of the yard.

Bolan had left a thin trail of gasoline leading from the storeroom. He scraped a match to life on his thumbnail and dropped the small flame at his feet.

As fast as a bolt of lightning, a tongue of fire streaked for the open doors of the small building.

For a moment there was nothing... then the volatile vapor rising from the tide of gasoline flooding throughout the building ignited in a single galvanic flash. A blazing fireball erupted from each end of the store. The roof fell in with a roar of flame, sending sparks whirling skyward. With the roar of the explosion still ringing in their ears, the two men heard the gasoline drums detonate one after the other. Within seconds the entire building was an inferno, a fiery holocaust spiraling a great column of crimsoned smoke hundreds of feet into the air.

The roof of the house was ablaze as well, and flames had appeared in all the upper windows. "Well, I guess we made our point," Mannering said. He turned and strode across the yard.

Three of the defenders—part of the group sheltering behind the trailer—were still alive. One sat cursing as he clutched a shattered shoulder, another was tying a bandage around a wound in his thigh. The third moaned softly, bloodied hands clawing a split belly through which a bluish heave of intestines showed. "I'm letting you bastards live," Mannering rasped. He spoke to the guy with the leg wound. "You know who I am. I'm leaving you alive so you can pass on a message to your bosses. Tell them I'll be back if they don't pack it in." With that the two men disappeared into the darkness.

6

The *American Dream* was a 35,000-ton luxury cruise liner with limited cargo facilities. She had been designed for the Caribbean trade. To help the rich tourists forget the violence threatening them on every side at the end of the twentieth century, she'd been fitted out in the overripe art nouveau style characterizing the end of the nineteenth. Mack Bolan felt as out of place in these surroundings as a quarterback at a board meeting. He was thankful when the ship dropped anchor off La Guairá, the port for Caracas, Venezuela, and they could go ashore.

"The mission here is strictly burglarious," Mannering told him. "I want to steal official files containing intel on the drug trade."

Heavy rain was falling as they stepped ashore from the launch, and the wooded hills inland were lost in low cloud. Mannering rented a Chevrolet Blazer with a pickup body and metal grille protecting the headlights and radiator. "This vehicle is more useful than a limo if there's a chase and we have to take to the hills," he murmured as he signed papers and paid the rental fee. "Especially in this kind of weather."

"Just who do you think would be chasing us?" Bolan asked.

"The secret police," he was told succinctly.

Caracas, no more than six miles from the coast, was a city of contrasts. Half the population was on the breadline; a small proportion of the rest had grown crazy-rich from the Maracaibo oil fields two hundred miles to the west. The highway ran past chemical works, a refinery, textile factories and then, on the outskirts of town, hundreds of acres of tin-roof shantytowns constructed from oil drums, packing cases and discarded lumber, where dispossessed peasants migrating from the coffee, cacao and sugarcane plantations in the Andes foothills waited in vain for work.

"Imagine a kid growing up in that," Mannering said, pointing at a group of ragged urchins wrestling in a sea of yellow mud that separated two rows of shacks. "Wouldn't you opt for a life of crime?"

Bolan creased his brow in a thoughtful frown, but made no comment.

They drove past a colossal semicircular apartment building with jutting balconies, then turned into an avenue of red-roofed white houses sandwiched between a huge domed church and a black-glass office building. The security HQ Mannering wanted to raid lay behind iron gates at the far end of the avenue. They cruised by then took a narrow lane that ran behind it. Mannering stopped the Blazer close to a high brick wall.

Bolan was studying a street map and a carefully drawn floor plan. "Once we're over this wall," Mannering said, "we can approach the place from the rear. We should be able to—"

"Not we," Bolan interrupted. "Me."

"What do you mean 'me'? With two of us, there'll be a much better—"

"No way," Bolan interrupted. "You don't have experience in this sort of hit, and having you along could very likely get us both killed.

"I have the plan," the warrior went on, "and I know what we're looking for. Look, I've done this before. All I need you for is backup. Without that, it's strictly no deal, okay?"

"Well, if you really think . . ."

"Just leave it to me," the Executioner said.

He handed Mannering the street map. "You can't park and wait for me. Someone could get suspicious. Keep the vehicle moving and pick me up when the job's done."

"Yeah, but how will I know—"

"You cruise around the neighborhood," Bolan said patiently, "keeping away from the main drags, and you work it so that you take this lane and pass this wall exactly on each quarter hour, starting at 1500. That's forty minutes from now. I'll fix it so that I'm waiting here on one of those quarter hours."

Mannering shrugged. "If that's the way you want it."

"It's the only way."

Bolan checked to make sure that the lane was deserted. The brick wall ran for more than half its length. The buildings on the far side could be warehouses or offices. There were no apartment buildings from which curious eyes could be watching, and the offices would remain empty until three-thirty or four o'clock. He climbed out of the cab of the Blazer, scrambled onto the roof, then dragged himself to the top of the wall. Mannering started the engine of the Blazer and drove away.

The Executioner was three feet above the sloping, shingled roof of an outbuilding. Beyond this, an ornamental fountain in the center of a courtyard was flanked by the tall white police building. An annex on the far side of the yard was linked to the main block by a glassed-in bridge. A black Mercedes limo was parked underneath.

Bolan's target was the annex. He glanced at the shuttered windows on either side of the bridge. As far as he could see, none sheltered a watching figure from the rain. He moved cautiously down the slant of wet shingles and dropped the ten feet to the ground.

Nobody shouted a warning; he heard no challenging voice.

A eucalyptus tree grew near the annex wall, its trunk surrounded by the white trumpets of catalpa flowers. Bolan sprinted across the courtyard and plunged in among the foliage. He jumped for a branch of the tree, hung swinging for a moment, then hauled himself up among the aromatic leaves. Seconds later he stepped onto the curved asphalt roofing the bridge.

From there it was an easy climb to the flat roof of the annex, but this was the point of maximum danger— while he was upright on the bridge, he'd be visible to anyone on the far side of the main street through the tall grillwork of the courtyard's entrance gates.

He drew a deep breath, flexed his knees and leaped for the stone coping at the edge of the roof.

Bolan gained the flat roof safely. The office he wanted was diagonally across, beneath the far corner, backing on the lane. The window, Mannering had told him, was set back behind a broad ledge, protected from burglars trying to break in from below by a spiked iron corolla at each end. But it seemed an intruder from above could lower himself unscathed.

Bolan lay flat and began to crawl forward. The street was deserted, and so was a small public garden beneath dripping trees on the far side. But either could become populated anytime. He figured there was less chance of discovery if he kept to the side nearest the lane and the empty warehouse and office building.

Once he gained the protection of an air-conditioning unit, the warrior uncoiled a rope from around his waist and studied the section of roof between him and the corner of the building he was aiming for. The color was identical but it looked smoother, somehow colder than the concrete. The rain pounding down on the area—it was about ten feet square—sounded different.

He tested the roofing carefully with one foot. It could be steel plating, and a sheet of steel could produce a noise like distant thunder however carefully you trod. But it seemed rigid enough, and there was no spring to it, as there would have been if it was painted steel. He decided to crawl across rather then go around. Skirting it, he'd be visible against the sullen sky to anyone in the lane. Moving slowly, he shuffled out from behind cover.

The world exploded around him.

The surface was toughened glass, a light-providing panel that must have been painted over for security reasons when the secret police requisitioned the building. Bolan's muscular two hundred pounds shivered the huge pane. It cracked straight across, then shattered. The warrior plummeted to the floor below.

The clatter of fragmented glass seemed to go on forever. Pieces were still dropping onto Bolan's back and shoulders as he rose dizzily to his feet. Miraculously he was unhurt. A knee was bruised, and a scar from his previous dive through a window had reopened and leaked a trickle of blood down his cheek. But no bones were broken and he was lucky—lucky that a large portion of the pane had collapsed, and not just a small area that would have cut him to ribbons as he flashed through the jagged hole.

The big man looked around him. Low clouds scurried across the serrated hole in the ceiling. He seemed to be in an outer office of some sort. IBM machines under plastic covers sat on top of a row of desks; steel filing cabinets lined one wall; papers were piled high in wire trays. Fragments of glass were everywhere, littering the desks, among the papers, crunching under his feet as he walked. A bell also rang insistently.

He realized it had been ringing for some time. It was obvious that he'd broken an alarm circuit when he fell through.

Bolan swore. There was nothing he could do about it now. If there was an alarm sounding, he'd have to come up with something that would explain the alarm in this specific place, a reason unconnected with his own unexpected entry.

He looked up. Could heat have caused a glass ceiling to expand and implode that way? It might just be possible, or at least believable enough to buy him the time he needed.

The room contained half a dozen cane wastepaper baskets. He emptied the contents in a heap beneath the hole in the roof and fired the pile with a match. When the flames were going well, drawn upward by the rising hot air and fanned by the draft blowing through the hole, he added the baskets themselves, a set of draperies dragged down from the rods above the shuttered windows and an armful of cardboard files that he found in a desk drawer. Finally he dropped in the coil of rope, which had fallen with him. He wasn't going to need it anymore, and it would help make the smoke denser once it started to smolder.

Coughing, the Executioner fought his way through the choking fumes and made the door. He eased it open, slipped into an empty corridor, locked the door and dropped the key in his pocket. He ran down the corridor to the office at the far end, where the information Mannering wanted was supposed to be filed.

The door wasn't locked, nor were the green metal filing cabinets beyond the paper-strewn desk inside. As far as the officials who used the room were concerned, there was no reason why they should be locked; the room served as a reference and clearing point for those concerned with the men employed by the secret police undercover section. The accountant who paid their salaries and expenses filed his paperwork here. The officers concerned with their grades, qualifications and contacts filed the information in this office. But there was nothing particularly secret about any of this. It was routine police secretarial material. The big safe built into the wall behind the door housed the real secrets.

Bolan wasn't interested in the safe. The intel that Mannering required concerned established contacts between undercover officials and the Colombian and Venezuelan drug barons. It would be invaluable to narcotics prevention authorities, as a possible blackmail lever, and as a guide to the secret route the trade used to link growers and users. It would be filed, Mannering said, under the names of certain Venezuelan police chiefs. He had given Bolan seven names.

It was eleven minutes before the roar and crackle from the locked office down the corridor was drowned by the clamor of bells and sirens in the street. Long before that, the feet of security guards pounded along the hallway. Bolan had heard shouts, the rattle of the door handle, the splintering of panels as the guards broke in—and the sudden increase in the fury of the fire when the air from the corridor fanned the flames.

Nobody thought to check the accountant's office. The firefighters and security men were concentrating on the room where the burglar alarm had sounded. Later, someone would think of the files and the safe. Later, too, they would start asking themselves how the fire started, and where was the person responsible. For the moment all was confusion.

The Executioner worked quickly. He knew he had very little time. First he leafed swiftly through a hand-written alphabetical directory on the desk, which told him which filing cabinets to open. He slid out only four drawers. Rifling through the folders inside, he selected one each from the first three and four from the last, shaking the papers they contained onto the desk. From each of the seven sheaves of typescript, handwritten notes and computer printout, he removed an index card lined in red. Each card listed a name, age, grade, and work history, with a passport-style photo stapled to the top lefthand corner. The neatly typed lines of text were followed by an eleven-figure reference number. Mannering would know what these code symbols signified.

Bolan tore the cards from the sheets to which they were attached and stuffed them into an inner pocket. He looked around the room.

A raincoat and slouch hat hung on a hook behind the door. He stripped off his parka and put them on. The raincoat was short in the sleeves, but it would have to do.

Setting off the alarm had stymied all his contingency plans—every step of the way had to be played by ear from here on. The noise from the hallway was increasing. He jerked open the desk drawers one by one. In the third he found what he was looking for—a pair of black-lensed sunglasses with heavy frames.

He put on the shades, turned up the collar of the raincoat and went out into the corridor.

At first he couldn't see a thing. The place was full of black smoke, and the lenses cut down his vision still more. But gradually he made out the figures of men with axes and a hose, and the flicker of flame amid the smoke. He shouldered his way through, the brim of his hat pulled low and his chin tucked into his collar. A man in a uniform barred his route.

Bolan had grabbed three boxes of files before he left the office. "Out of my way," he grated. "These files must be taken to a safe place."

Intimidated, the man pressed back against the wall, as Bolan passed.

There was a hallway at the far end of the passage, with stairs that led down past double glass doors to the street level. The covered bridge linking the annex with the headquarters building ran off a mezzanine. As the Executioner hesitated, the deflated fire hose, which ran past the open doors from a red fire pump angled in to the sidewalk, suddenly swelled and tautened. From behind he heard more orders shouted, and the hiss of water under pressure. Anytime now they were going to find out how trivial the fire was. He ran down the steps toward the street, where a crowd had gathered—guards with machine pistols, firefighters, rubberneckers and two policemen who had run across from the HQ. But beyond them there was space to maneuver. If he took the bridge, he could find himself trapped in unfamiliar territory. He had no floor plan of the headquarters building.

The guards conversed excitedly. Their weapons were still slung. Most of the other men seemed to be wondering whether to enter the annex. Bolan made no attempt to avoid them. The Colt, cocked, was in the right-hand pocket of the raincoat. But he believed that an air of authority, of arrogance, would carry a determined man past almost any officials where there was no actual ID check in progress.

He was right, too. He stopped in midstride by a fire chief bright with gold leaf and snapped, ''Get those men in there, for God's sake! We need every one. There's secret material at risk.''

The chief snapped a salute and yelled at his men. In Caracas, a man never knew which tyrannical bastard might next be in charge of his department.

Bolan turned his back on the cops, who were staring at the smoke rolling out through the open doors, and stepped onto the sidewalk.

He might have gotten away with it in another minute or so, but a man had just jumped out of a black Lincoln Continental, shouting something about secret papers in a safe to the chauffeur who was holding open the door for him.

The man was a heavily built, muscular guy with a beard—Raul Ortiz.

7

It was impossible to say who was the more surprised, Ortiz or the Executioner.

Face-to-face on the sidewalk, Ortiz realized instantly that the features of the tall man wearing sunglasses weren't Hispanic, that his skin was the wrong color, that the hat and raincoat were his own. Automatically, even if he didn't at once recognize Bolan, his hand dived between the lapels of his cream seersucker jacket.

Bolan triggered the Colt and fired through the raincoat pocket before his adversary's automatic was fully drawn.

The Colombian's eyes opened wide. He coughed a little blood, and then, as if the bones in his legs had suddenly been removed, he spun and collapsed face down beside his limo in the gutter. For a moment the rainwater gurgling past crimsoned, then it paled to a subdued pink as the blood diluted and was swept down a sewer grating.

The warrior was off and running, already halfway to the corner. The crack of the pistol shot, muffled by the cloth of the raincoat, had scarcely been noticed among the shouts of the men milling on the annex stairs. But the guards were alerted when Ortiz fell. One of the men behind Bolan let loose with a machine pistol, the burst of 9 mm slugs scoring the wall of the building as the warrior dodged out of range. He dropped the files, dragged the Colt from his pocket and fired a couple of rounds to discourage pursuit as he made the corner. Then he was sprinting up the side road toward the lane.

He turned into the lane and stopped, panting. The Blazer was accelerating toward him.

The warrior stepped into the narrow road and waved Mannering down. From behind, the sounds of pursuit neared the corner. If he could jump aboard while the Blazer was still moving fairly fast, they might be able to streak away before the gunners were close enough to score.

He readied himself for the effort, but the Blazer, its horn blaring, swerved around him and raced away toward the city center. He had a fleeting glimpse of Mannering's face set in grimly determined lines over the wheel, and then the vehicle was gone.

Bolan was taken aback and wondered what was going on. Then he hit on the answer.

He hadn't been waiting by the wall, so Mannering had barreled past the strange figure in the hat and raincoat.

To Mannering, a guy wearing a slouch hat, raincoat and shades in back of a secret police HQ could only mean bad news. Particularly if he had heard the shooting.

In a way, what had just happened wasn't so bad. The Blazer—Bolan thought, scrambling over a seven-foot wall beyond the warehouses—wouldn't in any way be associated with the fugitive who had taken on Ortiz in front of the annex. It would be a good blind once the roadblocks were set up, whereas, had he been seen jumping it, the Blazer would have been a death warrant on wheels.

Since nobody would now be on the lookout for the Chevrolet, all he had to do was dump the disguise and try to intercept Manning somewhere on his round. That way at least they would have a chance.

Bolan dropped into a backyard stinking with garbage and ran for the open door of what looked like a flophouse. They would need all the chances they could get—even if the police didn't know the intruders were connected with the luxury liner anchored out in the bay.

Once inside the hallway beyond the door of the building, the big man stripped off the hat, the raincoat and the dark glasses, and stuffed them in a malodorous space beneath a flight of stairs. He could hear shouted orders and the tramp of feet from the far side of the wall he had climbed. Intercept Mannering was fine . . . but where? Did he approach the lane the same way each time, or did he vary the route, using the street map in the pickup?

It was impossible to hazard a guess. The corridor led straight to an entrance door with panes of crudely colored glass filling the two upper panels. He catfooted to the door and listened. From the floors above, he could hear hushed voices, the creak of floorboards and certain other movements. The street outside was quiet.

He opened the door and was confronted with a young woman standing on the stoop. She wore high-heeled boots and tightly belted, shiny black rain slicker. With her left hand she held a transparent plastic umbrella over her head. A key on a chain dangled from her right.

She didn't favor Bolan with a glance as he came out the building. Johns who had already paid for one of the other chicks scored zero in a working girl's book.

He was on the bottom step when he saw the two Jeeps turn onto the street. They cruised slowly toward him, one on either side of the road, disregarding traffic coming the other way. As the Jeep on Bolan's side of the street drew near, he swung back to face the hustler, leaning her way with an arm braced against the brick-work framing the door. He stood on the step, his head level with her own.

"Honey," he said, "you look so good I just got my second wind. How much?"

Bolan didn't register the price she quoted. He was too much aware of the low-gear whine of the Jeep passing behind him. He knew South American cops—if they were merely suspicious that someone had committed an illegal act they were capable of shooting that person in the back. He waited tensely until the Jeep was several houses away.

He reached for his wallet. "Come to think of it, I really don't have the time. Sorry." He handed her several bills.

The girl shrugged and watched him walk away. Americans!

At the next intersection, Bolan ran down a flight of steps into a warren of narrow streets that webbed a low-lying area between two broad tree-lined avenues. It was around here that Mannering should be circling with his map.

Right on. When he was fifteen yards from the mouth of a long, winding alley, Bolan saw the Blazer drive slowly past along a cross street. He risked a shout, but Mannering didn't hear him. When he got to the corner, the vehicle was two hundred yards away, turning left.

The Executioner swore. Mannering was on his way to make the second pass behind police headquarters. In the quarter hour since the first, they wouldn't have had time to organize many checkpoints; in thirty minutes, when the Blazer passed again, they could have every street sewn up.

Bolan decided on a risk. The important thing was to join up before the guy was on his fourth or fifth pass. Mannering was a guy who placed a high price on efficiency and organization. Bolan was going to gamble on that. He'd stay right where he was, in the shelter of the alley, counting on the SAFE director to take the cross street once more in a quarter of an hour.

It was the longest fifteen minutes in the Executioner's life.

He found a doorway behind an evil-smelling row of trash cans and drew back into the shadows as far as he could. The rain pelted on the cobbles and swirled down the center of the alley, carrying empty cigarette packs, orange peels and scraps of paper. Occasionally traffic swished past along the street. In the distance he could hear music, and once he saw a Jeep pass the end of the lane. The hands of his watch crawled.

Seconds before Mannering was due, the Executioner walked to the mouth of the alley. A bus passed down the street, spraying out a fan of water. Then he saw the Blazer. It was traveling quite slowly, on the far side of the road. It seemed the most natural thing in the world to step out and signal it to stop.

"What happened? What the hell are you doing here?" Mannering demanded. "Did you get the cards?"

Bolan climbed in and slammed the door. "Yeah. What happened to *you*, the second time you made it down the lane?"

"I didn't," Mannering said. He pulled out past a tanker and accelerated toward a street market tarped against the rain. "Some spook tried to stop me the first time, and I figured it'd be safer to wait at the end. But I didn't see any sign of you.''

"You did the first time," Bolan rejoined. "I was the spook."

Mannering turned his head to stare. "No kidding? So tell me—what *happened*, for God's sake?"

Bolan told him.

They had left the modernistic apartment buildings of the Avenida Romulo Betancourt and taken a feeder road that led to the highway linking the capital with the port when they saw the first roadblock.

Half a dozen cars waited in line on the near side of a striped barrier pole, a panel truck and a bus on the other. Three militiamen were checking papers and searching the first car while a couple of uniformed police carrying submachine guns stood by.

"Put your foot down and drive straight through," Bolan instructed.

Mannering stared at him. "But there's nothing wrong with our papers. We're from the cruise ship. Shouldn't we try—"

"They're searching the people as well as the cars. If we have to turn out our pockets and they find those file cards . . ." Bolan didn't have to finish the statement.

"Maybe you have a point at that," Mannering conceded. Clenching his teeth, he shifted down, approaching the line of stationery vehicles, then abruptly swerved into the center of the road and raced for the pole.

They had about one hundred and fifty feet to travel. Needles spun around the Blazer's dials; the engine howled. Before they were halfway there the noise got through to the militiamen, who fell back from the car they were searching, not believing that the Blazer would really smash into the barrier. The militiamen had their submachine guns leveled and ready to fire. They didn't need beliefs.

Bolan saw the points of fire flicker from the perforated barrels. The Blazer lurched as a stream of heavy slugs plowed into the radiator grille and suspension. The windshield starred and shattered. Mannering smashed his fist through the toughened glass in front of him and drove on.

The Executioner rolled down the passenger-side window, leaned his wrist on the sill and aimed the Desert Eagle. He had no intention of killing law-enforcement officers doing their duty, even if their orders came from the secret police. He fired over their heads, hoping the blast and muzzle-flash of the awesome Magnum would scare them off their aim.

The tactic worked. Along with the militiamen they dropped to the ground or leaped behind the first car in the line. They fired again from the new positions, but by that time the pickup was level and past, zooming for the barrier at fifty miles per hour.

The grille struck the wooden pole almost in the center, snapping it in two like a matchstick and sending the halves spinning into the air.

Mannering sawed at the wheel, skidding the vehicle past the halted panel truck with shrieking tires. The pickup skated broadside onto the road, was overcorrected, then laid down rubber, snaking toward the highway.

Through the rear window Bolan saw policemen running for a Jeep, one of whom was holding a walkie-talkie to his mouth. "There'll be more," Bolan said tightly. "We better pour it on."

Mannering nodded. Three minutes later he gunned the Blazer into the double traffic stream speeding along La Guairá highway.

Twice Bolan thought he saw the Jeep in among the press of buses, trucks and cars on their way to the port. Once he was sure he heard the wail of a siren. "Take the next turnoff," he told Mannering. "Even if the traffic's too dense for them to catch up from behind, there'll sure as hell be roadblocks ahead."

The hollow boom of the Blazer's 5-liter V8 engine snarled up the scale as Mannering shifted down, shifted again and zigzagged between the fast-moving vehicles to the inside lane. He braked in front of a giant semi hauling a forty-ton container of refrigerated meat, ignored the trucker's angry horn blasts, and shot down a ramp that tunneled beneath the highway and emerged in a residential area to the west.

The blacktop looped up a hillside studded with expensive villas. Fifty yards from an intersection at the top, the Blazer's engine coughed and died.

Bolan jumped to the ground. Several gunshots had pierced the gas tank, and the fuel had leaked out. "No problem," he reassured Mannering. "With a smashed windshield and bullet holes all over, we had to ditch her anyway. We'll take a walk and grab a cab."

Nobody challenged them as they trudged off through the rain.

A quarter of a mile later they came across a shopping mall with covered walkways, an underground parking lot and security men at every corner.

Bolan went into a boutique selling exotic fruits and bought a large varied selection. Mannering visited a liquor store and came out with half a dozen bottles of fiery local specialities. In a men's room shining with copper and white porcelain each stashed his weapons beneath the produce in the grocery sacks. Then they went to look for a cab.

A line of cars for hire was outside the mall. The cabbie was talkative, and favored them with a rundown on Venezuelan politics since the discovery of oil.

There was a checkpoint where the road rejoined the highway, but getting past posed no problem—the cabbie knew the two soldiers who advanced on each side of his vehicle, submachine guns up and ready. Rich Americans from the cruise ship, he told them, spending their dollars up the hill. He reached a hand into the rear of the cab for their passports, steamer tickets and shore passes, handing these through the window to the soldier on his side. The man flicked through them, handed them back and waved the cab on.

End of story.

Bolan and Mannering made the last shuttle ferrying passengers back to the ship. They were in their staterooms by six-thirty.

Half an hour later, the *American Dream* weighed anchor and sailed for Fort-de-France, in the French West Indies.

Bolan and Mannering installed themselves in the art nouveau dining room at eight o'clock. Waiters fussed and swooped. The sommelier pursed his lips over a bottle of claret someone had dared to send back. Women chattered about the prices in Caracas. Dinner appeared to be proceeding in the normal way, except that the captain wasn't seated at the head of his table.

It wasn't until eight-thirty-five, when the claws and shell of the lobster thermidor were being cleared away, that there was a warning chime from the ship's PA system.

And then the captain's voice, strained and shaky, announced that the *American Dream* had been hijacked, and was now in the hands of Central American revolutionaries.

8

The hijack had been well planned and expertly carried out. Like most good ideas, it was simple. In the early afternoon, a lighter loaded with merchandise destined for Fort-de-France, on the French island of Martinique, had moored alongside the *American Dream*. The cargo—textiles and light-engineering machine tools— was packed into six-by-four wooden crates, which were hoisted aboard by derricks and stowed in the forward hold while most of the ship's passengers were ashore.

The terrorists were smuggled aboard inside some of the crates.

There were seventy crates in all. Four of them concealed three hijackers each, packed lengthwise and separated by polystyrene baffles. A fifth case was packed with weapons and explosives.

As soon as the cruise liner put to sea, the twelve men operated quick-release catches and emerged into the hold. They opened the fifth crate, armed themselves, and made their way to the bridge. They were very well informed—within fifteen minutes the captain, the chief engineer, the radio operator and every senior officer were held at gunpoint.

The captain's announcement over the ship's intercom system caused consternation among the passengers, most of whom were elderly. A woman screamed, another fainted after a bout of hysterics. Bolan and Mannering exchanged glances and said nothing. They were two against . . . how many? Action had to wait until they had more information.

"I am ordered to instruct you all, crew as well as passengers," the relayed voice continued, "to assemble in the ballroom on C Deck, where you will be given notice of what is expected of you."

There was a pause, interrupted only by the crackle of static, and then the captain's voice, shakier still, went on, "I am further commanded to say that . . . that any passenger or crew member disobeying the instructions that will be given in the ballroom will be shot on sight."

After an amplified click, the dining room was left to the outraged, and now frightened, mutterings of passengers and stewards.

Three men had appeared inside the double glass doors that led to the dining room. They were Hispanic, about thirty years old, and wore military fatigues and long-peaked caps. Each carried a submachine gun and toted a bandolier filled with 9 mm rounds.

"All right," the tallest of the three shouted. "You heard the orders. Down to the ballroom now, all of you, on the double!"

The three SMGs were raised menacingly. Pushing, jostling, complaining, with some of the women crying, the hostages left their tables and crowded out the doors. Two more armed terrorists waited outside to escort them.

A white-haired man with fierce blue eyes and a bristly mustache stormed up to the tall terrorist. "This is outrageous!" he fumed in a deep voice rich with Southern vowels. He wagged a finger in the terrorist's face.

"We're on an American ship here, and I'm telling you—"

"Shut up."

"Who the hell do you people think you are? Some band of illiterate, unprincipled bandits who—"

"I said shut up. Do what I say or I'll shoot you," the hijacker threatened.

"You will not. You're not going to get away with this, you son of a—"

"Do what he says!" someone shouted from the rear of the crowd pressing toward the doors.

He was too late. The Southerner's furious tirade was cut off in midsentence by a short, sharp eruption of gunfire.

Blood spurted scarlet from between the shoulder blades of the passenger's white tuxedo. He sat down very suddenly, then flopped over on his back with red flowers blooming on his shirtfront, his blue eyes staring sightlessly at the ornate ceiling.

Amid the cries of horror and indignation, a woman shrieked and flung herself toward the fallen man. She was seized by the two other terrorists and hustled into the corridor outside. The killer wedged the toe of a combat boot under the body and tipped it over onto its face. "Get rid of this," he ordered his confederates. "Over the side."

Bolan's lips tightened in frustration and fury; his fingers itched to feel the heavy butt of the Desert Eagle cached in his stateroom. He logged the scene in his memory. He would present the bill and demand payment later.

Below in the ballroom, two curlicued sections of the paneled wall had been slid aside to reveal the bandstand. The tall hijacker, flanked by his two lieutenants, stood center stage—a bizarre trio in front of the sheeted piano, the empty music racks and cymbaled complex of the drummer's kit.

"I tell you the way things're going to be," the tall man said. "I'm only going to tell you once, so you better listen good, eh? Go back to your cabins and staterooms and stay there. The stewards have orders to lock you in. Once each day they'll bring you food. But they'll be covered when they come, so don't step out of line. Once each day those of you who don't have private facilities will be escorted to the washroom. But hear me—we got plenty of guys here, and more will come aboard tonight. This ship will be patrolled, and anyone, but anyone, seen outside of their cabin or without their escort will be dusted. On sight, no questions asked. You read me?"

A confused murmur ran through the assembled passengers and crew members, then a man in back called out, "Can I ask a question?"

"Try me."

"It's just . . . well, what are your demands? There are some pretty influential people aboard, and if it's money, well maybe we could—"

"No demands," the hijacker interrupted brusquely. "We need the ship. You people are hostages held against the aim of the authorities to take it away from us. Why we need it doesn't concern you."

"This food-in-the-cabins routine," a white-jacketed steward asked, "how the hell can we—"

"We'll attend to you guys later. You muster in the kitchens and we'll talk, okay? All you need to know now is that the food is to be staggered, deck by deck, companionway by companionway, throughout the day. With our guys to keep things cool."

After a short silence, the hijacker added, "Right. That's it. Now, move your asses. Get out of here. Fast."

A rattle of bolts from the two men beside him and the pair still standing guard in the passageway outside underlined the urgency of the order. With no sound but the shuffle of feet and the deep, distant thrumming of the liner's engines, the crowd dispersed.

"WAIT," Mack Bolan said. "That's all we can do right now—wait and see what goes down. It's useless to try anything until we know who they are, how many they are and how strong they are. All we know at the moment is that they're pros."

"What kind? Holy War terrorists? Commies?" Mannering had been strangely silent since the captain's first PA announcement.

"Not for my money," Bolan replied. "You know guns. How do you read their weapons?"

"The SMGs? They're Heckler & Koch MP-5s."

"Right. And what does that tell you?"

Mannering scratched his chin. "Don't know. It's a compact, accurate weapon. The West Germans arm their police and border guards with them, and then—"

"Yeah. The West Germans. In my book, the Arab terrorists, the Red Brigades, any of the far left extremists, all use Kalashnikovs, Stechkins, any of the stuff the Russians are so quick to hand out to troublemakers that side of the line."

"And these guys are Hispanics. The tall bastard speaks with an accent, could be Mex. You're saying they're on the far *right*? I mean like the Contras, that kind of thing?"

"Something like that," Bolan said. He stared out the port. Their stateroom was on the Promenade Deck, and he could still see, very faintly, the lights of the Venezuelan coast through the rain. "But we're wasting our time, trying to read the situation, until we have more intel."

Bolan could have picked the lock on the stateroom door in less than two minutes. But there was no point exploring the empty public rooms and deserted corridors while the ship was at sea; no point engaging the terrorist commandos in a running gunfight; no point at all in giving away the fact that they had weapons—at least not until they knew a lot more about the hijackers' MO, their aims and how many of them there were.

During the night, Bolan had heard the whine of a turbojet and the clatter of rotors. In the distance men were shouting. He thought the language was Spanish, but the throbbing of the engines, the creak of woodwork, the bulkheads' amplification of all the small sounds characteristic of a ship riding the swell, distorted the words and he couldn't be sure.

The rotor noise grew louder, then steadied. The chopper was hovering over the ship. Bolan guessed it must be transferring aboard the reinforcements the hijacker had spoken of. As far as he could tell from the audio evidence, the bird was poised over the foredeck, probably above the hatches that covered the hold, where there was plenty of space. He looked out the stateroom window again, pressing his face to the pane and shading out the room's reflection with one hand. But the Promenade Deck lighting had been extinguished and the glass was pockmarked with raindrops. He could see nothing.

At nine-thirty the next morning, the door was unlocked and their cabin steward, a New Yorker named Flanagan, came in with a tray carrying plates, forks, glasses and a single covered dish. A man they hadn't seen before stood on guard outside with an MP-5.

"You've got to make this last until tomorrow," Flanagan said, setting the tray on a table. "One delivery a day is all we're allowed."

"You're moving around, Flanagan," Bolan said swiftly in a low voice. "You must hear these people talk. Who are they? What do they want? What have you and the other stewards found out?"

"Not a damn thing, sir, and that's the truth," the steward replied. "They only used the radio once so far, and none of us was near enough to hear. Nobody called back, and Tiny Watson—he's the chief steward, sir— Tiny said that must mean they'd put out no ransom demand yet. But they're Central Americans, all right. They were joking about the situation, and I heard one guy say this would help them get the Communists out of their country at last."

"Did he say what country?"

But before Flanagan could answer, the guard stepped into the stateroom. "No talking!" he snapped. "Come. The next cabin now."

Mannering was looking at the tray. "There are no knives here," he complained.

"No, sir. Our...friends feared they might be used as weapons."

"And what are we supposed to drink?" Mannering gestured toward the empty glasses.

The guard growled something in Spanish. Bolan translated. "He said we could learn to use the faucets."

"I HAVE NO IDEA where they come from," Hal Brognola said to the presidential aide. "You tell me. All we know is that the ship's been taken over. No announcement has been made, no ransom terms and no demand for the release of political prisoners broadcast.''

"How do you know the ship *has* been hijacked?''

"The radio officer had time to initiate a mayday call. He only got a few words out before it was interrupted by the sound of a shot. Since then, there's been none of the usual ship-to-shore exchanges.''

"And nothing at all from the terrorist side?''

"We have one radio intercept,'' Brognola said. "In Spanish, in some kind of verbal code. The code breakers read it as meaning the ship will continue to call at the cruise ports as advertised—don't ask me why. Plus there was an indication they might be receiving an arms shipment somewhere along the line.''

"An arms shipment?'' the aide repeated with raised eyebrows. "These guys are always armed to the teeth anyway. I'd read that as an indication they were aiming to meet up with friends and start some sort of action someplace.''

"Me, too. But there's no hint of how or where. The call wasn't answered, and it hasn't been repeated. It could have been picked up anywhere in the Caribbean.''

"You've tried to raise the hijackers?''

"Naturally. Zero response.'' Brognola sighed. He cleared his throat. "George, what does the President want me to do?''

The aide was examining his manicured nails. "Shadow the ship,'' he replied. "Keep her under close surveillance, at sea and at anchor. Stay in close contact with the local security people wherever she calls.''

"No rescue attempts? No operational plan to board the ship and dislodge these bastards? I ask because— entirely by chance—I have a contact on board."

"A contact? Who? A Company man? One of your group?"

"Just someone I know. But reliable."

"Let him be. Leave him there until we need him."

"So there's to be no action at all?"

"No action. Not until we know more. Specifically, until we know which side of the fence the terrorists jump." Choosing his words carefully, the aide added, "In the case of certain Central American states, the Administration might not, uh, be entirely out of sympathy with the political beliefs of organizations wishing to change the system of government in those countries. For the moment, therefore, we have to play the waiting game." He coughed. "Always provided, of course, that the safety of the passengers comes first."

"Of course," Brognola said dryly. "The passengers' safety has to come first."

9

"Don't fry your brain asking why, but we're going over the side once it's dark, and then we're going ashore," Mannering said. "There's business I have to attend to in the interior, and tonight's as good a time as any."

"Yeah, but we can't just abandon all these people."

"Who said anything about abandoning? I know where the powered life rafts are stashed, the ones that inflate as soon as they hit the water. We'll be back before dawn, ready to wake when Flanagan brings in the next meal."

Bolan was looking across the Promenade Deck. A police car was parked at the end of a stone pier, and two cops leaned against the fender and studied the *American Dream* through binoculars. "Whatever you say," he replied.

The warrior continued to stare through the porthole. Today the sky was cloudless, as blue as the sea that reflected a million points of sunlight. Half a mile offshore, a fleet of fishing boats creamed the water. What was his next move?

First he had to look at the situation objectively. What was the aim of the mission? Why was he on this ship? To help Mannering combat the escalating drug menace. And any success of Mannering's would be one step forward in his own unrelenting march toward the suppression of this evil, enslaving trade.

But now the liner had been hijacked by terrorists. The fight against terrorism, against all extremist action that put the lives of ordinary folks at risk, was as high on the Executioner's list of priorities as the drug battle.

Which campaign had priority here, the long-term or the short?

Should he ride out this insufferable inactivity, play the hijack by ear and hope it would sort itself out, with or without his help, as soon as possible, and then get on with the drug war? Or should he shelve Mannering's operation and concentrate on the terrorists?

Bolan's impatience with inactivity swayed his decision. They would go overboard for the next skirmish in the antinarcotics crusade that night, and do their damnedest to help best the terrorists just as soon as they had enough intel to work with.

AS SOON AS IT WAS dark, Bolan said, "Okay, let's go."

"You want to work on this lock?" Mannering stood by the cabin door.

The Executioner shook his head. "We don't know how often they patrol, whether they post guards at the corners, and even a slight noise could alert someone, especially if it's around a cabin door."

"Then how—"

Bolan gestured at the outer wall. The opening, half porthole, half picture window, was a rectangle with rounded corners. It was three feet wide, with a hinged panel above that opened inward for ventilation. Even with the struts removed and the panel dropped, the space wasn't deep enough for a big man to pass through. Mannering looked puzzled.

"This way," Bolan said, "we can at least see out. We know who's watching and who isn't. We'll lift out the whole frame, and wedge it back in position while we're away." He produced a ring of small, bright, stainless steel tools and started to work on the frame.

Brass screws retaining the wood fillets came out first, followed by heavier screws that secured the thick metal window frame in the bulkhead aperture. After that it was a question of coaxing away the sealing compound before the whole unit could be lifted out. The operation took seventeen minutes, with a three-minute break while the patrol passed by. "They make it three times each hour," Bolan said. "I checked this afternoon. That means we have twenty minutes to climb out, replace the window and hit the road."

To allow themselves the maximum time, they waited until the patrol's next round and then, once the hijackers were out of sight, removed the weighty frame, scrambled onto the deck and maneuvered the frame back into position. "It's not one hundred percent secure," Bolan said, "but killing the deck lights helps us more than them. Unless they turn a flashlight on it, we should be okay."

"Unless the ship puts to sea and there's a heavy swell," Mannering muttered.

"If the ship puts to sea," Bolan rejoined, "you and I will be left behind. For my money, she won't. There's no sign of presailing drill up forward."

They stared each way along the dark, deserted deck. Beyond the rail, black water reflected the harbor lights and illuminations beyond the quays. "Which way are your rafts?" Bolan whispered.

"Aft. In a big locker beneath the last lifeboat. You may need those tools again to open it."

"No problem. But first we check out the whole deck," the big man said. "I like to know the enemy positions before I act."

They stole forward, under the white-painted timbers roofing the shelter deck, beneath the port bridge wing, until they stood on the edge of the space immediately below the wheelhouse and navigation bridge, and above the cargo hatches.

The area was well lighted, the space bright as an empty stage. "We can't risk crossing to the other side," Mannering muttered. "Look." He jerked a thumb at the prow.

On the foredeck, in the shadows beside the windlass, two tiny spots of red pinpointed the cigarettes of lookouts stationed there to survey the sector forward of the upper works, and the sea to port and starboard.

The davits from which the first of the lifeboats was slung were on the edge of the open space. Bolan motioned Mannering to stay where he was and darted into the shadow between the boat's keel and the rail. He turned, squinting back and up.

There was light behind the windows of the wheelhouse and bridge. Above the crow's nest, which topped the streamlined foremast, the ship's radar scanner revolved ceaselessly beneath the stars.

Bolan could see shadowy figures moving behind the windows. Several men paced up and down, arms waving as they talked. The terrorist chiefs planning their next move? A discussion with the captive officers on the next phase of the voyage? Reaction, maybe, to some reply to a ransom demand?

Questions with no answers. The guys on the bridge were occupied, was what mattered. They wouldn't be busting their skulls wondering who was doing what on each deck; they would leave the patrols to take care of that. Bolan dropped flat and crawled back to Mannering. "We'll check out the stern, then the other side."

At one point, leaning over the rail, they could see a two-man patrol tramping the circuit of B Deck below. Passing an open doorway, they checked out a guard with an SMG standing at the intersection of two passageways.

Three or four hijackers were gathered beneath an awning, aft of the swimming pool, joking and laughing. Bolan knew the routine—the Castros, the Guevaras, they were dead serious about their "revolutionary missions," so everyone else had to be serious, too. Or dead. But once the hired help were off the leash, they like to fool around just like ordinary human beings. As he watched, the hijackers moved to a hatchway and vanished on their way to a saloon on the deck below. "Right," Bolan said. "The locker."

The locker was five or six feet square, its lid secured with a hasp and padlock that took the Executioner all of twenty seconds to spring open.

The life rafts were bulky, folded into thick packs. They were heavy, too, with the cylindrical motors attached. "What kind of power packs are these?" Bolan asked.

"Electric. Very modern," Mannering replied. "Basically the same as the ones frogmen use to tow them around under water. With a battery life just over a couple hours."

A section of the rail beyond the locker hinged outward. Below this an accommodation ladder slanted down the side of the hull toward the sea. The lower half of the ladder was stowed horizontally, leaving a gap of twenty feet between the last rung and the surface of the water. "You dive?" Bolan asked.

Mannering nodded.

"Let's go."

The raft, he reckoned, would make too much noise—enough maybe to alert the gunners on the foredeck—if they flung it over the rail. It would be better to manhandle it down to the foot of the ladder and drop it directly the shorter distance.

It took them a quarter of an hour. Once they had to freeze halfway down the accommodation ladder when the patrol passed above. But finally they made it and let go thankfully of the pack. Both men were sweating.

Compressed air hissed into the rubberized fabric as soon as the raft hit water, and the chambers started at once to swell and inflate. Bolan and Mannering dived in after it.

They heaved themselves aboard and allowed the raft to drift slowly along the liner's hull until it was below the stern. They could hear no sound but the slap of wavelets against the anchored ship's steel plates, and a distant blare of music from some waterfront bar. Mannering switched on the electric motor and the raft hummed quietly away, out beyond the huge dark bulk of the *American Dream*, away from the breakwater and the harbor lights.

The rubber gunwales bulged and flexed as they hit a slight swell. "You said we were going ashore," Bolan said.

"Affirmative. Fort-de-France lies on the northern shore of a big, irregular inlet. The bay's more than five miles deep and five across. We're heading across, due south, to a place called Les Trois-Îlets. The three islands."

"You got contacts there? Friends?"

Mannering was looking ahead, gazing at a distant string of lights, blurred by distance and the darkness, that rose into view every time the raft topped a swell. "Friends?" he repeated. "Well, people I know, anyway."

Bolan remained silent. He was letting the guy make the pace. Mannering knew the island; he didn't. Mannering was into the illegal narcotics scene here; he wasn't. As long as they were still on the antidrug beat he was content to play the waiting game and handle the cards the way they were dealt. For the time being.

There were ships anchored across the inlet mouth—at least two corvettes, an ocean-going cruiser and a French coast guard cutter like the one Bolan had seen from the stateroom. None of them showed any lights. Evidently Bolan's wasn't the only waiting game.

Mannering kept the powered raft a half mile inshore from the marine cordon. The surveillance teams were unlikely to be scanning their radar screens when their target rode quietly at anchor off Fort-de-France, in full view of the lookouts. And in any case the electric motor's signature, if it showed at all, would be so low-profile that it would be almost indecipherable. In direct vision at that distance, on a moonless night, the raft would be invisible, rising and falling with the swell.

The crossing took them just over one hour. By the time Mannering ran the unwieldy craft in beside a breakwater jutting out from a private beach, the warm subtropical breeze had dried their clothes on their bodies. Bolan unzippered his waterproofed neoprene pouch, took out his two guns and reholstered them. Mannering had left the Walther behind. It was too difficult to conceal, he'd said. He stuffed the Combat

Master in the waistband of his pants, where it would be hidden by his seersucker jacket.

A concrete ramp ran alongside the breakwater. Mannering jumped ashore and tied up the raft. Bolan cut the motor and joined him.

The beach bit into a spit of land that ran out west of the town. Beyond shrub clumps and a row of palms, the pale shape of a flat-roofed villa was visible. On the far side of the spit, the lights of Les Trois-Îlets varnished the sky with a yellow haze.

Mannering led the way up a slope of close-cropped grass. "There should be a vehicle waiting for us in the carport," he murmured.

There was. As they rounded the corner of the shuttered house, they heard the sudden roar of a gunned engine, and the vehicle, with headlights blazing, careered straight at them along a concrete driveway. Flame belched from the rear of the speeding vehicle, a fierce cannonade of submachine gun fire that ripped through shrubbery leaves and drilled into the trunks of palms.

Bolan was flat on his face in a shallow ditch bordering the drive when the Jeep screeched around in a broadside and raced back toward the villa for a second pass. His fighter's instinct, some sight or sound beyond his consciousness, had alerted him in the millisecond before the lights flared to life, and he was hurling himself sideways by the time the first volley ruptured the silence. But it had been a near thing—the neoprene pouch was torn from his belt, and one steel-jacketed messenger of death had come so close that he felt the wind of its passage on his cheek.

Both his hands were wrapped around the Colt—the smaller gun's muzzle-flash was less evident than the Desert Eagle's—but he held his fire until the Jeep was twenty yards away. Then he pumped four shots in rapid succession at the open rear of the vehicle. At the same time, the deep-throated boom of the Combat Master showed that Hillyard Mannering was alive and well and shooting from the far side of the concrete strip.

In the instant before the Jeep disappeared around the corner of the building, one of the gunners in back uttered a choked cry and spun off into the driveway. His submachine gun clattered to the ground as he fell. Bolan saw, in the fading back reflection of the Jeep's headlights, that the guy was struggling to his knees, reaching for the weapon. Then Mannering decked him forever with two more rounds from the Combat Master.

The light brightened again . . . from behind the Executioner. The killers were making a complete tour of the villa and attacking from the other side.

The warrior scrambled to his feet, ran across the driveway and snatched up the SMG. The pistol grip was still warm from the dead man's grasp. He flung himself down beside Mannering as the Jeep reappeared and bounced toward them over the slope of grass.

Bolan raised the stuttergun and shot out the vehicle's headlights. He lowered the barrel to shoot at the front tires, but after one final burp the magazine was exhausted. He threw the gun away and drew the Desert Eagle. "You go left. I'll go right," he whispered to Mannering. With death in each hand, he stole through the bushes.

Mannering clicked a fresh magazine into his weapon and vanished in the direction of the villa.

The Jeep was still coming at them. In the sudden darkness, the driver shifted down, shifted again—then the engine screamed, and the vehicle fell over onto its side on the steeply slanting lawn, its tires hit, perhaps, by the burst from Bolan's gun.

It had been crewed by only three men—the driver and the two gunners in back. The survivors leaped for safety and dropped down behind their capsized transport.

Creeping through the shrubbery, Bolan was already in a position to enfilade. He didn't know where Mannering was. He crouched now, waiting for a sound or a movement.

For a moment there was neither; the gunners had no targets. Suddenly, amid a rasp of static, an amplified voice spoke unintelligibly into the dark. Bolan frowned. He couldn't make out the words, but the language was French. If the attackers were using one of the normal CB frequencies, they were running a big risk.

Or Mannering and the Executioner had run into a very big-time deal indeed.

The SAFE director threw a clay flowerpot into the bushes fifteen yards to his left, not far from his previous position. The men behind the Jeep fell for the ruse. Both gunners opened up, one with his SMG, the other with a revolver.

Mannering got off several shots that found their marks. There was no more gunfire from behind the overturned Jeep.

Bolan approached the vehicle and cautiously turned over the bodies. They were young guys, wearing bush shirts and khaki pants. "Hell!" Bolan exploded, examining the dead men's papers with a penlight. "These guys were plainclothes policemen from the local antidrug squad!"

"I wouldn't be surprised," Mannering said. "Cops can be bought—here like anyplace else."

"I draw the line at fighting soldiers of the same side. Corrupt or not."

"I don't have such scruples. The drug barons pay the cops to keep guys like us off their backs. As far as I'm concerned, the cops here are fair game. C'mon. The vehicle meant for us should still be in the carport on the other side of the villa."

They had been provided with a brand-new Ford Bronco. The keys were in the ignition.

Mannering climbed behind the wheel. "We have to burn rubber if we're going to make the boat before dawn," he said. "The place we have to go is near Rivière-Pilote—not much over ten miles, but these are rough, twisty mountain roads."

"Yeah," Bolan said, "and if the past is a model for the future, there's bound to be opposition."

10

"Okay, they were cops," Bolan said when they had driven away from the villa and reached the highway. "But how could they have known you'd be there at that time?"

"A leak," Mannering said briefly. "Happens all the time."

"Sure, but whoever leaked the intel must have known you'd be landing at that time, at that particular place, on this night. How could they have? We only decided to take that raft a couple hours ago ourselves."

"The liner's on schedule still," Mannering replied. "If she hadn't been hijacked, she'd have anchored here tonight anyway. And if she hadn't been hijacked, we'd have gone ashore in the normal way. I'd have rented a small motorboat, made the same trip and landed here around the same time. The arrangements had been made, we were on schedule too. And they were waiting for us because of this leak."

"What about your contacts, the guys who left this Bronco for us? You figure the cops on someone's payroll took them out?"

"Search me." Mannering shrugged. "Maybe we'll find out when we make the rendezvous."

They bypassed the picturesque fishing port, climbed through banana and sugarcane plantations and passed a distillery where the cloying odor of rum spiced the air. The road skirted the flank of an extinct volcano and rose again to a wooded upland fifteen hundred feet about sea level. Two miles from the town of Rivière-Salée, the blacktop swerved away to the left and the Bronco bucked onto a dirt road that spiraled toward a bare ridge.

"I wasn't sure until now," Bolan said two minutes later, "but we've got a tail."

Hunched over the wheel, Mannering nodded. "Four headlights, two white and inner ones yellow," he agreed. "I've been watching in the mirror."

"Let's gain a little distance, then pull off the road, hide and jump them."

"Good idea. If they're part of the same team, and the guys at the villa wised them up before we took them out—or if there was a backup unit watching from a distance—they could already have radioed ahead to set up another roadblock."

"Okay," Bolan said. "As soon as you like."

They were traveling along a comparatively straight section of road. At the far end, the trail dipped into a shallow valley, over a bridge that spanned a stream, then climbed again to lose itself among the broad leaves of a banana plantation. By the bridge a forest track, still muddy from the previous day's rain, snaked away along the riverbank and then vanished in the depths of a wood. Mannering shifted down and swung off the dirt road. The tires scrabbled on the muddy surface, sawing the vehicle from side to side.

The headlight beams revealed a torrent of dirty yellow water. The trail followed it for two hundred yards, then dived through a ford and twisted away between banks of head-high tropical undergrowth.

Mannering rocketed the Bronco through the ford, sending huge swathes of water fanning out on either side. Twenty yards farther on, the engine choked and died.

He cursed, turning the key. The engine spun, wheezed, but wouldn't start. "Shit!" Mannering exploded. "Goddamn water was deeper than I thought. It must have shorted the ignition."

Over the rushing of the stream, they heard sounds of the approaching pursuit vehicle as the driver shifted down for the bridge. "They'll spot us as soon as they make the next straightaway," Bolan said tersely. Through the trees, they saw the lights of the car as it howled up the grade on the far side of the valley. "We better get going."

"Yeah," Mannering agreed. "Once they see we lost the Bronco, they'll deploy through these woods like bees over a bed of flowers."

Half running, half walking, they splashed along the trail, using the penlight as a guide. The land rose for a quarter of a mile, then began dropping toward another valley. Eight minutes after they quit the Bronco, light lanced through the wood behind them. Distant shouts and a low-gear grind indicated their escape route had been discovered.

"If they're professionals," Bolan said, "they'll spread out into the woods around the Bronco. But for my money they'd also send a car with a radio along this track. You still figure this for a drug-squad operation?"

Mannering shook his head. "No idea. Depends where the leak was."

"You still want to make your rendezvous?"

"Damn right. We don't have far to go."

"Is the exact timing of the meet important?"

"Not one bit. The other party doesn't know we're coming."

"I see," Bolan said. He strode a few paces in silence. Then, "So we shake off the tail first."

"Right."

The forest trail twisted suddenly and ran out into an open space. They were looking down a stubbled slope at a large plantation house surrounded by floodlighted outbuildings. Beyond it, a narrow blacktop ran straight as a die through hundreds of acres of sugarcane. Where the road began to rise there was more light, diffuse, apparently moving, above the tall crop.

"We'll make it," Bolan decided. "There could be transport we could use."

They plowed across the field with soft, wet earth sucking at their feet. The house was white, with slated shutters and a veranda that slanted out beneath fretted wood balconies on the second floor.

Bolan and Mannering stopped on a grass patch behind a barrier of tree ferns, peering across the yard. Someone had just backed a Land Rover from a barn and left it beneath a frangipani tree. Inside the barn, they heard another engine start—more powerful by the sound of it, with a stressed quality and a crackle to the exhaust gases escaping from the muffler. Bolan drew the Colt and looked over his shoulder. The woods they had left were backlighted, but there were no pursuers in sight.

The second vehicle to emerge from the barn was a small Peugeot sedan. But it was the high-performance GTi version, with a souped-up engine and rally tires. They crouched, ready to make their move when the little car stopped. From shrubbery on the far side of the yard, the night wind wafted spicy scents of cinnamon and orange blossom.

The Peugeot wheeled around until it faced the road that ran through the plantation. A thin middle-aged man wearing gold-rimmed glasses climbed out and walked toward the barn, leaving the engine running. He reached for the barn door.

"Close the door and walk with it," Bolan said softly behind the man. "This is the muzzle of a Colt Elite automatic, and it's loaded. If you don't want to get hurt, pull the second door shut and stay inside."

The guy scarcely paused in his walk. He shut the door, took hold of the heavy bolt on the other and backed into the dark interior, dragging it after him. Mannering was already in the Peugeot's passenger seat.

Bolan glanced at the house. The upper windows were shuttered and there was nobody on the lamplighted veranda. He followed the man into the barn. "Turn around," he said in the gloom.

The thin man licked his lips. "Look," he said, "there's no need to—"

"I'm not going to kill you. Turn around."

Reluctantly the man turned. "I'm sorry about this," Bolan said as he raised the gun butt and struck a blow that rendered the man unconscious.

Bolan slipped out the door and sprinted for the car. The light among the trees was much brighter, and he thought he saw silhouetted figures moving. "We'll be partially hidden by the tree ferns," he said. "And they might not know it's us in this car. Depends how long they've been looking this way."

He slammed the lever into first and stomped hard on the pedal. With a small shriek of tires, the Peugeot shot forward and arrowed along the road between the sugarcane rows.

"They're halfway down the field," Mannering reported before the plantation cut off his view, "but it's heavy going in the mud. Couple of guys with SMGs are walking beside a Jeep, which looks kind of crowded. There's no way of telling if they're on to us."

"They have to check out the farm," Bolan said. "By the time they've done that we'll be long gone, whether they're on to us or not."

For almost a mile, the straight, narrow road climbed toward the summit of a rise in the land. A few hundred yards from the house, a tractor with an overhead light was working a clearing in the plantation. Black workers wielding machetes loaded cut cane onto a trailer. The tractor driver, recognizing the car, waved at them as they passed. "Night harvesting," Mannering said. "Making up for yesterday's rain. Or maybe they have a contract with a penalty clause."

By the time they made the crest, the Peugeot was hitting the mid-seventies in third. No headlights were visible down the long perspective of macadam behind them. Bolan eased the GTi into fourth, and they plummeted down into an undulating landscape over which the dark plantation stretched as far as the eye could see. For fifteen minutes, they snaked through the vast estate, between high green walls of vegetation.

Finally, rounding a sharp curve, Mannering exclaimed, "I got it! I knew the lay of the land was familiar! This must be the road... I always wondered where that blacktop led!"

Bolan lifted his foot. The cane thickets had given way to the huge, broad, spear-shaped leaves of banana trees. "You know where we are?"

"Sure do. Unless I'm mistaken, there's an intersection around the next corner where this road joins the one we left. All we have to do then is backtrack a couple miles and we're there."

"Where?"

"The place we're going," Mannering replied.

Bolan compressed his lips. "You'll need to fill me in on what's going down," he said evenly.

"Don't worry. I will."

Mannering was right about the intersection. Bolan swung onto the familiar dirt surface and followed the road through the woods. A few moments later Mannering said, "Okay. Slow down. Kill the lights."

Bolan complied. Sudden darkness, then the trail gradually emerged as a pale ribbon curling away ahead. "There's a couple hundred yards of meadow beyond the trees," Mannering said, "and then we drop into a hollow. The place is down there on the right. I'd like to stash the car at the top of the grade—there's some kind of a shack we can leave it behind—and then continue on foot."

"Whatever you say." The Executioner feathered the accelerator pedal, allowing the little sedan to drive itself quietly in second.

The shack was set back from the road, a dilapidated wooden ruin that looked as if, once, it might have sheltered workers from the weather. Bolan steered the Peugeot behind the shack and switched the engine off. "Okay, let's have it," he said.

Mannering eased open the door, motioned the warrior out, then led him to the top of the grade.

A complex of tall farm buildings stood in a grove of cypress trees below them. Bolan could see the faint glint of starlight on automobile bodywork in front of the main entrance. He reckoned there were at least three vehicles there. Between the farmhouse and one of the outbuildings he made out the rectangular mass of a parked shipping container.

"There's four tons of cannabis resin in that trailer," Mannering told him, "destined for the U.S. market. They grow the weed here. Out back they got fields of opium poppy. Not as good as Triangle material, but good enough. A high-tech lab for refining heroin is hidden under the floor of the smallest barn."

"And we're here to hit the place?"

"You got it."

"I don't have much faith in the success of assaults where the attackers start out with no intel, no planning."

"No sweat. We'll look the place over and work on a plan when we know what the score is," Mannering told him.

"We already hit one place, burned a year's supply of cocaine and got away with it. Seems to me we were lucky on that one. Could be that our luck has run out. We could wreck the laboratory, but how do you destroy four tons of hash? Burn it, and have the locals for miles around stoned out of their minds?"

"It's a farm," Mannering said. "They'll have pesticide sprays, weed killer, nitrate fertilizers. We don't have to obliterate the shit. We spill it out the container, foul it up, make it unusable, is all."

The Executioner wasn't happy with Mannering's unplanned, off-the-cuff action. It went against all his instincts, countered all the lessons of experience. "This is a valuable commodity," he said, "like gold. Don't you think the owners might have security?"

"Sure they will," Mannering said confidently. "But we've got firepower, and we've got the element of surprise. We'll look the place over first, and then we'll bust in and take them."

"You've been here before, I take it," Bolan said as they made their way downhill.

"Yeah. I've passed by several times. They've got a front, of course. Place works as a regular farm. Sugarcane, bananas, a little coffee, that kind of stuff. That's why there's no chain-link fence around the property, no guard dogs, nothing outwardly to distinguish the place from other farms around here."

"Who runs it—members of the cartel?"

"Medellín connections," Mannering agreed.

They left the road fifty yards above the farm complex and began a slow circuit of the property, at first ducked down beneath the umbrella fronds of banana trees and then, as they worked around behind, in among the rows of sugarcane. From the slope where they walked, they could see an extensive yard separating the three-story farmhouse from a cluster of four barns in the form of a letter *E*. Light showed in two of the second-floor windows of the house and beneath the tall double doors of the smallest barn.

"They work day and night in that underground lab," Mannering murmured.

Crop-spraying machines, tractors, a mechanical harrow and several small flatbed trailers were parked against the outer wall of the longest barn. The container was nearer the house.

When Mannering and the Executioner reached the road again, they turned around to retrace their steps twenty yards nearer the buildings. Level with the machines, Mannering whispered, "If we climbed onto a tractor and smashed through the entrance doors—"

Glaring light dissolved the darkness and dazzled them with its brilliance.

Bolan cursed, dropping to the ground. The white light blazed out from floods beneath the roofline of each building, illuminating in stark detail the farmhouse, the yard, the barns and bare earth as far as the bananas and the sugarcane. They'd tripped a magic-eye burglar alarm that automatically lighted the area when the beam was crossed.

Mannering was prone beside the Executioner with his Combat Master in his fist. "Stay exactly where you are. Make a move and you're dead men," a harsh voice called from somewhere behind the lights.

Bolan glanced over his shoulder. They were completely exposed, lying on a slope of bare earth with twenty yards of nothing between them and the cane thicket behind, another fifteen separating them from the machines, the barn wall and the nearest cover in front.

"Don't try it," the voice warned again. "There are guns all around you."

The subsonic reports were scarcely audible, but rounds from at least four, perhaps five silenced weapons scuffed up the dirt in a neat rectangle enclosing the two intruders.

"Okay, you made your point," Bolan called.

"Throw your weapons out in front of you, then wait right there," the voice instructed.

Bolan tossed the Colt; Mannering followed suit with his pistol.

Within seconds, several men appeared from behind, frisking them as they lay there. Bolan's belt, shoulder rig and the Desert Eagle were removed. A man in camouflage fatigues scooped up the two jettisoned guns. "On your feet now and walk, slowly, toward the house," the unseen man ordered.

Without turning his head, Bolan reckoned there were still four or five men in a tight half circle behind them as they approached a rear entrance to the farmhouse. "Inside," the leader grated, "and I want your hands clasped, pressing the back of the neck."

"Bring them here," a new voice called from inside the house, "and we'll see what we caught in the net."

Bolan couldn't place it exactly, but he thought the voice sounded familiar. After being hustled through a second doorway with Mannering, he saw why.

The bearded man seated at the far end of a long scrubbed table was Raul Ortiz.

His left arm was in a cast, supported by a sling. Between the edges of a plaid wool shirt open to the waist, bandages that encircled his ribs were visible. His face was pale and his cheeks hollow, but the eyes beneath his black brows glittered dangerously.

"So," he said softly, his eyes widening in recognition, "my old friend from the Snowman. And of course from a certain office in Caracas." His gaze switched to the ring of gunners behind the two captives. "Keep these two men very well covered, Marco. I have a score to settle with the tall one. What did you find on them?"

A swarthy roughneck wearing blue jeans and a sleeveless denim jacket tossed the three guns and a bunch of ID documents on the table.

Ortiz scanned the papers. "Belasko, eh?" the bearded drug baron grunted. "A photographer." He laughed, but there was not a lot of humor in the sound.

"I'll allow you're a fucking snooper, but it's the first time I saw a newshawk with a .44 caliber camera!"

"You got me," Bolan said. "Let's not kid ourselves. I'm here—"

"I know why you're here," Ortiz interrupted. "And I know who you're with, and why. You've been caught with your pants down, the two of you. You're both armed, and you're in trespass. The supposition would be that you were preparing to commit a criminal offense."

"So call the cops and make a complaint," Mannering suggested.

"Now that isn't exactly what I had in mind, to tell the truth," Ortiz said.

"What *did* you have in mind?" Mannering asked huskily.

"Since you inquire, asshole, I'll tell you." The Colombian was suddenly genial. "Friends of mine—Sicilian friends—stateside thought up some dandy ways of taking care of folks in their time. One guy they stripped, shoved a meat hook between his shoulder blades and hung him up in the cold storage along with the other carcasses. They warmed him up some with a cattle prod so he'd jump around and sink the hook in deeper. But it still took him four days to die."

Bolan shot a sideways glance at Mannering. The guy was sweating.

"Another guy, they tied him in a chair and left him with a cloth soaked in pus from some tropical disease bound around his eyes. And a third case I heard of, they gagged a snooper with broken glass and then beat him around the face with a nightstick."

Ortiz grinned. "But I'm not going do anything uncivilized like that with you two. I'm going to let you sample the benefits of civilization. Face it, I'll be doing you a favor.

"In a favorite American movie of mine," he went on, "there's this cop, see, Gene Hackman, who's getting too close to the bad, bad drug suppliers. So what do they do? Instead of dusting him, they kidnap the guy and shoot him up until he becomes a hopeless addict himself."

Ortiz fixed his burning gaze on the Executioner. "You caused me a lot of trouble, friend. A lot of trouble, a lot of money, and—" a glance at the cast and the bandages "—a lot of pain."

"I hoped you'd be feeling no pain," Bolan said. "I hoped you were dead."

"Well, soon you'll be feeling no pain yourself, smartass. We're going to inject you so full of shit that by the time we turn you loose, maybe in two weeks time, you'll have to knock off Fort Knox before you can buy enough of the hard stuff to satisfy your addiction." Another smile. "Make the punishment fit the crime, don't they say? Now isn't that neat?"

For a moment there was silence. Mannering licked his lips. One of the gunners behind Bolan laughed.

Then Ortiz shoved back his chair, grating the legs on the brick floor. He levered himself upright with his good hand and unhooked a rubber-tipped cane from the chair back. "Okay," he said. "I have to go into town now, fix the times for the next shipment. I'll take Nini and Emilio with me. You, Marco—take these creeps below for their first shot. A heavy dose, but watch out that they don't OD. Guy and Bertrand here can help keep them quiet."

He limped around to the far end of the table. Mannering and the Executioner were still standing with their hands linked behind their heads. "I'm going to enjoy seeing that glazed look in your eyes when I get back," Ortiz said to Bolan. "Believe me, it'll be a pleasure. A real pleasure." Without warning, he raised the stick and slashed the big man viciously across the side of the head.

The impact rocked Bolan back on his heels. The blow raised an angry welt on his face.

"I'll remember that," Bolan grated through clenched teeth.

"I want you to remember it, you bastard," the Colombian hissed. "I want you to remember it when you're sprawled on the sidewalk in your own puke, crying for a fix you don't have bread enough to buy."

"I'll see you in hell first," Bolan said.

"You'll be in hell, all right, but you won't see me!" Ortiz chuckled and stomped from the room. Two of the gunmen followed him. A moment later Bolan heard a car start and drive away.

"Okay. Outside," Marco barked. Bolan turned. The two gunmen looked tough. One was tall and thin, with a drooping mustache and a seamed and expressionless face. The other man was shorter, bulkier, but all muscle, with a slit mouth and a blue-stubbled chin that looked as if it had been hacked from a block of granite. Each carried a silenced Ingram machine pistol. Marco's spatulate, black-rimmed fingers were clasped around the butt of a mini-Uzi.

From the accent and the name, Bolan figured Marco for Hispanic. The others could have been local French.

Bolan took a chance. Speaking very quickly, from the corner of his mouth, he said, "Follow my lead. Don't start anything. Drop when I say."

"No talking, goddamn it!" Marco yelled. He raised a foot and shoved the base of the Executioner's spine. "Get going and shut up!"

The group of men walked out of the room and through the rear entrance door. In the yard, the lights still blazed. Mannering and the Executioner were prodded across to the smallest of the barns, where Marco thumped three times, then three times again, on the double doors.

They heard a heavy crash—a trapdoor flung open, Bolan thought—and then the sound of footsteps. One of the doors creaked open, and the man who stood there was wearing a surgical mask. He was about five-six, thin, pale, with black-framed pebble glasses pushed up on his forehead. "What gives, Marco?" he asked querulously. "You know I have this refining—"

"Button your lip, Professor," Marco ordered. "We have two customers for the purest of the pure—but carefully calculated. You better chase all that bad air out. Ventilate the noxious vapors and ready a nice clean syringe, okay?"

The chemist straightened the front of a white linen lab jacket and breathed out hard through his nose. "Very well," he said, "but if the consignment's late…" He shook his head and walked back toward the shaft of light streaming up through a rectangular trap in the barn floor. He climbed down a ladder and disappeared from view. Seconds later a mechanical humming pulsed through the barn. Bolan knew the by-products of heroin refinement could be toxic to breathe. He assumed the guy had cranked up some type of air-conditioning equipment.

"Down to the operating theater now." Marco grinned. "Bertrand, you make it first and keep our guests covered while they're on the ladder. The boss'd hate it like hell if they fell and hurt themselves."

The thin gunner with the drooping mustache lowered himself through the trap. Marco pushed Mannering forward. "You next."

"Can we lower our hands now?" Mannering asked. "You can't expect us to walk down a ladder with—"

"Okay, okay. But step out of line and you won't need the fix."

The SAFE director went down, followed by Bolan. Bertrand stood like a statue at the foot of the ladder, with the silenced Ingram trained on them. Guy, the muscular one, brought up the rear with Marco.

The laboratory was quite small, with white-tiled walls and a concrete floor. Bolan saw crucibles, retorts, burners and spirals of glass tubing on a central workbench. Stoppered jars of morphine base were arrayed on a second bench along one wall. He assumed the harvested capsules of the opium poppy would be drying upstairs in one of the barns.

At the far end of the laboratory was an office furnished with four filing cabinets, a desk and a leather visitor's chair. A fan whirred in a circular housing above the door.

"In there," Marco ordered, "and strip down to the waist, both of you."

Behind the desk, the chemist had produced cotton swabs, a bottle of colorless alcohol and two lengths of rubber tubing. He opened a drawer and took out a hypodermic syringe and small transparent sachets containing a crystalline white powder. "What's the dose?" he asked.

"Heavy," Marco said. "But not terminal."

"I better check pulses and heartbeats," the chemist said. A stethoscope, a spoon and a small Bunsen burner joined the objects on the desk.

Mannering had removed his seersucker jacket and shirt. He was trembling. "Take his arms and hold him, you guys," Marco ordered. "I'll keep this one under control while the Professor shoots." He stood off to one side with the Uzi leveled at Bolan's belly.

Bertrand and Guy moved to seize Mannering's arms. Bolan pulled his shirt over his head. As he shook his head free, the shirt fell to the floor. He bent to pick it up, yelling suddenly to Mannering, *"Drop!"*

Mannering went as limp as a rag doll, plummeting to the concrete floor to evade the gunners' outstretched arms. At the same time Bolan whipped out the short, broad-bladed throwing knife strapped to the inside of his left ankle and flicked it at Marco underhand, with all the steely strength of his wrist.

The razor-sharp blade sliced through Marco's throat, just beneath the jawbone. The gunner uttered an animal cry, at once choked off by the fountain of blood gushing from his mouth and the wound. He hit the floor at the same time as the Uzi.

Bolan was already on the move. Following through the swing of his knife hand, he launched himself in a football tackle at Bertrand's knees.

Hit by two hundred pounds of bone and muscle, the gunman staggered sideways, involuntarily grabbing Guy for support. Both the Ingrams had been slung, as the hardmen were using their two hands to grab Mannering. Before they could disentangle themselves and reach for the machine pistols, the Executioner had leaped to his feet.

His arms wrapped around Bertrand like the jaws of a bear trap, pinioning him in a viselike grip. For perhaps half a second they teetered together, the tough, wiry hardman using every ounce of his strength in an attempt to shake Bolan off. The warrior leaned back, the muscles of his forearms as rigid as iron hawsers, and lifted Bertrand's heels from the floor. He banged the guy's feet up and down while his fingers searched for and found the Ingram's trigger. Short bursts of lead sprayed the walls and ceiling as they struggled.

Guy had steadied his own weapon, but hesitated to fire in case he shot his buddy.

Mannering raced across the floor and scooped up the dead man's Uzi. He rolled over on his back to line up the stubby barrel on Guy as the gunner gritted his teeth and pumped a short burst a couple of inches to one side of Bertrand. But Bolan was swinging the thin man around, and the slugs missed him and tore away the upper part of Bertrand's arm.

The man screamed, relaxing enough in shock to allow the Executioner to jerk up the Ingram's barrel and fire a burst into his body. Bolan let go, and Bertrand's body dropped to the floor.

Mannering fired the mini-Uzi. After the silenced thumps of the Ingrams, the stutter of the diminutive machine pistol was appallingly loud. Guy stayed upright under the impact of the 9 mm slugs, then collapsed.

It was then that Bolan saw the chemist taking a small nickeled automatic from one of the desk drawers. He hurled himself across the desk, sweeping off bottle, syringe and sachets, to slam the drawer on the man's hand. The chemist yelled in pain. Then, before Bolan could stop him, Mannering fired again—a long eruptive burst that punched the frail chemist back against the wall. He slid lifeless to the ground, leaving a broad crimson smear on the white tiles behind him.

Mannering scrambled to his feet, laughing a little hysterically. "Teamwork, Belasko!" he cried.

"Let's go," Bolan said soberly, "before Ortiz and his friends find us."

11

"What's the latest on the hijack?" Bolan asked the bartender polishing glasses in the waterfront café at Les Trois-Îlets.

It was late. Other than two fishermen waiting to take their boats out a couple hours before dawn on the high tide, the place was empty. "Don't you read the papers?"

Bolan shook his head. "Been up-country," he said. "And no radio. The last I heard, some Central American revolutionaries had taken over the ship. Now they tell me she's anchored off Fort-de-France!"

"They told you right, man," the bartender replied. "All the passengers are locked in their cabins and don't get to eat more than once a day. Captain and crew have guns at their heads. That's what they say."

"What are the hijackers demanding?"

"Don't ask me," the bartender said. "Astolat's lighter was out there today with food supplies. Crates of merchandise, too, they tell me. But that's all I know. You want a four-star rundown, ask the police."

Bolan sipped his beer. Mannering was toying with a layered gray-and-vermilion drink that was known locally as a *perroquet*.

"If we want to be back aboard before daylight, I guess we better make tracks," Mannering said.

Bolan nodded. The sedan they had taken from the farm was parked a block away. He drained his glass and put money on the counter. A panel truck pulled up outside the bar with a squeal of brakes, and the driver, without leaving his seat, tossed a bundle of newspapers onto the sidewalk.

The bartender opened a flap in the counter, walked through to collect the package and cut the string holding it together. He put the papers down beside the espresso coffee machine at one end of the counter. Bolan bought a copy and scanned the front page.

The headline spread across five columns, but the piece beneath it was short.

Police, coast guard and military units were keeping watch at dawn today as the hijacked cruise liner *American Dream* remained anchored off Fort-de-France with no sign of imminent departure.

There was no sign, either, of any immediate action to board the ship, subdue the terrorists and free the 200 passengers and 50 crew members. Navy helicopters from the American fleet are keeping the liner under close surveillance, but although the majority of the hostages are U.S. citizens, armed interference by American forces is for the moment ruled out. "The situation is delicate," a Navy spokesman told this reporter. "Until we know more about the hijackers and their demands, precipitate action could compromise an eventual solution and put the lives of hostages at risk."

A source at the police department at Fort-de-France revealed late last night that no specific conditions for the release of the prisoners had been received. Only one message from the terrorists had been transmitted, the source said, and this had threatened that passengers would be killed one by one and, if necessary, the ship blown up, unless the voyage of the liner was allowed to continue without interruption. One passenger had already been murdered during the initial takeover of the vessel.

Rumors current in Caribbean diplomatic circles suggest that the terrorists, who have not so far identified themselves, may be extreme right wing activists interested in overthrowing the leftist government in an unnamed Central American country. There is speculation that certain supplies— which the hijackers have insisted be taken aboard without any official inspection—may in fact be arms destined for this purpose.

Seized off Caracas (Venezuela) three days ago, the *American Dream . . .*

The rest of the article was recap. Bolan folded the paper and left it on a sidewalk table. "Doesn't get us much farther," said Mannering, who had been reading over his shoulder.

"No," Bolan agreed, "but it gives us more time. If they're making some kind of a round trip, picking up arms shipments on the way, we might get a chance for some action back on board. Especially if your own business is finished now."

"It isn't," Mannering said. "We have things to do in Rio. And again in Port-au-Prince, Haiti, on the way back."

"If the ship does follow the original cruise plan," Bolan said.

They picked up the car and drove to the private beach on the far side of the promontory where they had left the raft. Bolan pondered, as he drove, the ambiguous personality of his companion. Mannering had been hell-bent for the attack on the farm in Colombia; he had been brave—if foolhardy and inexperienced—during the assault itself. In Caracas, despite an initial attempt to share the dangers with the Executioner, he'd been content to take a back seat. The hijack of the liner saw him totally subdued, and when they were being threatened by Ortiz, Bolan could have sworn the guy was scared. Yet he fought well, surprised by the ambush; and he had killed the chemist without compunction where Bolan would have preferred to save him and ask questions.

The different components of the man's personality—as far as they had been shown to Bolan—didn't quite stack up. Somewhere, the warrior felt, there was an extra piece of the puzzle he hadn't yet seen.

The Executioner's unease was growing. He'd have to keep his eyes wide open the next few days.

A curving residential street led downhill to the villa. They saw the lights around the empty house as they topped the rise—a flashing amber light on the roof of an ambulance, revolving blue police lights, a flood illuminating the overturned Jeep. Torchlights moved among the bushes as cops searched the grounds. A gravelly voice issued orders over a patrol car radio.

"Neighbors must have alerted them when they heard the gunfire," Bolan said, "and they've been here ever since, picking up shell cases and measuring footprints."

"I hope to Christ they didn't find the raft."

"No reason for them to look shoreward," Bolan replied. "There'll be tracks left by the Bronco. They'll read it as a battle between cops and robbers, and the robbers took off."

He cut the lights and coasted the vehicle to a stop in a line of cars parked outside a hotel at the top of the hill. They took the weapons and ID papers they had recovered from the farm, added a coil of rope Bolan had discovered in a barn and stole down between two clapboard holiday homes to the beach on the far side of the spit. "It would be safer," Bolan whispered, "if we swam around the point and approached the raft from the sea."

The water was warm. A salt breeze ruffled the surface, spiced with the faint perfume of sea pinks and tamarisk.

The private landing stage on the far side of the promontory was in darkness. No guards were silhouetted against the lights at the top of the slope. Hidden beneath the breakwater and the ramp that ran beside it, the raft still bobbed gently on the swell.

Mannering cast off, and they heaved themselves out of the water, flopped over the rubber gunwales and lay prone. "The tide's ebbing now," Bolan said in a low voice. "We'll let it carry us out a quarter of a mile before we switch on the motor."

False dawn was beginning to pale the sky above the conical hills of the island when the raft floated beneath the high stern of the *American Dream*. The ship was entirely silent. Mannering coaxed the craft in under the stowed accommodation ladder while the Executioner prepared to swing up the weighted rope and drop it between two steps on the counterbalanced lower section.

It was difficult trying to stand upright on the raft's rubber floor, and it wasn't until the fourth attempt that the lead eye at the end of the rope dropped through and they could haul the ladder down to sea level. Each time the rope-swathed lead hit the ironwork, it seemed to them that the metallic boom would awaken the whole shop, but no guards appeared at the rail above and nobody challenged them as they climbed aloft.

Bolan left the raft's electric motor running. As he stepped onto the ladder, he shoved the craft away so that it headed for the open sea.

They were back in their stateroom with the window in place before daylight and the passage of the first Promenade Deck patrol.

"YOU'RE TELLING ME," Hal Brognola said angrily, "that whether or not we move to help these poor bastards depends entirely on what some chairbound Washington analyst makes of the hijackers' demands?"

"I'm telling you nothing," the presidential aide replied. "All I want to make clear is that any definitive decision that could in certain circumstances result in the establishment of an operational command must await evaluation of the status quo by the competent authorities."

"Christ," Brognola exploded, "you don't have to talk to me as if I were a press conference, George! What you mean, basically, is that if the terrorists turn out to be Communists, we hit them. But if their ultimate aim is to overthrow a Communist government someplace, then we discreetly lend a hand."

"Not 'a hand,'" the aide said. "Encouragement."

"In other words, you'll let them ship arms aboard as long as the target they'll be firing at meets with your approval."

"The safety of the passengers comes first," George said sanctimoniously, "and if that can be assured by allowing the hijackers certain maritime concessions, then I don't think the Administration would look unkindly on some kind of compromise."

"I wish to hell I could contact Striker," Brognola murmured.

12

The *American Dream* left Martinique at noon. Three of the hijackers came for Mannering sixty minutes later.

It was very hot. Beneath a cloudless, leaden sky bronzed fiercely by the sun, the ocean was calm and glassy. Churning south at a speed of thirty knots, the cruise liner creamed an arrowhead wake on the blue water that could be seen by the shadowing choppers fifteen miles behind.

Bolan and his companion were catching up on lost sleep when the stateroom door banged open and the terrorists trooped in. The men had been served the usual rice mixture at nine o'clock, but not by Flanagan, their usual cabin steward. When Bolan had asked where Flanagan was, the new man had shrugged and thrown an apprehensive glance over his shoulder at the armed terrorist outside the stateroom. Now the hijackers were inside—three beefy Hispanics with their Heckler & Koch SMGs trained steadily on the bunks at each side of the cabin.

"Okay," the man in the center of the trio growled. "Which of you is Mannering?"

Mannering sat up and swung his feet to the floor. He was wearing red-and-white-striped pajama pants with a scarlet silk Chinese robe embellished with black dragons. "I am. What do you want?"

"You're to come with us."

He stared. "What for? I don't understand. Why should—"

"No questions."

"But why—"

"Enough!"

Mannering opened his mouth to speak again, but the terrorist lowered the gun and slashed him backhanded across the face. The blow left four livid welts suffusing the skin. Blood welled slowly from a cut over the cheekbone, which was caused by a Mexican silver ring.

Involuntarily Bolan started forward, but another hijacker rammed the barrel of his MP-5 into the big man's stomach, momentarily doubling him over.

"Cool it," the man in the middle snapped, "or you'll be shark bait before you draw your next fucking breath."

He turned to Mannering. "You have to answer a few questions. We found out who you are. Save America from Evil, huh?" He laughed harshly. "Friends of ours in Colombia and Central America are getting pissed off at your kind."

"What do you say we save America from Mannering?" one of the other terrorists asked.

"It's a thought," the leader of the three admitted. "But right now the boss is eager for answers. If this jerk can supply the intel, maybe we can wise up our friends enough to kill the organization from the inside. Let's go."

The two subordinates seized Mannering by the arms and rushed him into the corridor. He shouted something to Bolan as he went, but the Executioner couldn't catch the words.

The man with the Mexican ring paused in the doorway. "You behave," he said, stabbing a forefinger Bolan's way.

The door closed; the key grated in the lock.

The stateroom seemed suddenly very empty. Glasses tinkled on the bathroom shelf and small objects on a night table chattered together as the whole fabric of the ship shuddered under the thrust of the engine-room turbines.

Bolan was seething with impatience, furious at the temporary impotence imposed on him by the situation.

Mannering had to be rescued, that was imperative. But even if he could free him from his captors, where could they go? There were a lot of hiding places on a big ship, but not many where two guys could stay indefinitely, not many that could be researched without running into patrols posted on every deck.

A patrol tramped past the stateroom window five minutes later, two stocky, clean-shaven men he hadn't seen before. How many hijackers were there? The three men who had taken Mannering, these two, two he'd seen patrolling before. There were four more on the two other main decks, a couple on the foredeck, at least two more at the stern and the gunner who'd murdered the passenger during the takeover. That was sixteen. How many more to guard the engineer, the captain and his officers? How many to keep the crew under control, to watch the cabin quarters?

Plenty! Bolan thought. At least twenty, more likely two dozen.

How best to help Mannering?

If the guy held out, it might be best to wait right here until after dark, when he'd have more freedom of movement, more chance to work unobserved. If they broke him, on the other hand, and he spilled the details of his relationship with the Executioner, they could be back in the cabin any time with orders to take Bolan.

He could cover both angles, he reckoned, if he wasn't there.

He waited for the patrol's next round, then eased the window out of its frame once more. While he was waiting he retrieved the weapons from their hiding places: the Combat Master and the Desert Eagle taped to the underside of the lid of the toilet tank; the Walther SMG strung to the wire springs beneath Mannering's bunk; his Colt and a small bag of spare ammunition clips pinned to the inside of the window draperies, up near the rods.

He was going to take the whole armory with him. The point of maximum danger was while he was transferring the pieces to the Promenade Deck with the window out of place. Running that close would be the few seconds it took him to make his chosen hiding place.

He had decided to lie low, until darkness fell, in the locker where the life rafts were stowed. The padlock would still be open. With one of the rafts missing, there would be room for a man to curl up, then lower the lid once he was in there.

Bolan listened with every sense alert for two full minutes. Beyond the rail, a foam hissed along the hull; the engines thrummed; a lifeboat creaked in its davits. On either side he could hear the voices of passengers confined in their cabins. A woman argued querulously; farther away a child was crying.

Satisfied no-man's-land was as quiet as it could be, he lowered the weapons carefully to the deck from the open window, then vaulted lightly through. It was much more difficult for one man to replace the frame than two, especially with the draperies drawn behind it, but finally he maneuvered the heavy unit into place and scooped up the guns. He was wearing blue jeans, a black turtleneck and sneakers.

He holstered his own two weapons, stuffed the Combat Master in the waistband of his jeans and carried the Walther. He padded quickly along below the lifeboats on the port side. At least two passengers, peering cautiously between drawn curtains, saw him.

Ten feet from the white locker, he dropped onto his hands and knees and crawled. There were, as he expected, two terrorists on the poop deck. If he had stayed upright any longer they would have spotted him. By the locker, he reached up his free hand and tested the cover, which lifted easily enough.

He heard a noise behind him and turned his head. A door in the deckhouse wall opened, and a hijacker stepped out onto the deck.

The man was tall and thin, with a pockmarked face and lank, greasy hair. He was wearing the customary combat fatigues but no peaked cap. He looked around forty years old.

Seeing Bolan sprawled on the deck, bristling with weaponry and about to open the locker, his mouth opened and his eyes widened. And he hesitated for a fraction of a second. Then the data logged by his sensory apparatus came up with a printout and his right hand streaked for the heavy automatic holstered on his hip.

Bolan had used that fraction of a second. He jerked up the Walther and squeezed off a short lethal burst.

The terrorist never got his gun free of its holster. He hinged forward, lips snarled back in a soundless scream, fell to his knees and vomited blood.

Bolan acted fast. The burst was no more than five or six shots, but it sounded like an artillery bombardment aboard the silent ship. He had used the Walther because he figured the familiar stutter might fool the hijackers into thinking one of their own men had fired on some passenger stepping out of line. But to make that stick he had to get rid of the body.

Still kneeling, he dragged the dead man toward the scuppers, raised him two-handed to the polished wood rail and pushed him over. The body dropped into the sea.

A spattered pool of blood was left behind on the deck, but there was no hope of cleaning it up. He looked hastily around. A stack of canvas-seated reclining deck chairs leaned against the deckhouse wall. Bolan grabbed several and piled them beside the locker and beneath the lifeboat. They could have been left there by a deck steward who'd been interrupted in his duties. And the congealing bloodstains were covered.

Since the shots, there had been shouting from all over. Because of some acoustic trick, added, perhaps, to the total surprise and the short duration of the burst, nobody seemed able to pinpoint the location of the gunfire.

"On B Deck, halfway along!"

"Hell, no. It was higher up, on the port side."

"I think it was the big saloon, at the foot of that companionway."

And then, from the bridge wing, "For God's sake quit fooling around! Move your asses and find out which of you fired and what was fired at."

Bolan grinned. It would take them some time to find out a man was missing, and even then they wouldn't know for sure that it wasn't *his* weapon that fired. Let them work it out. It suited him fine.

Cautiously he raised the locker lid high enough for him to squeeze in with his arsenal and hunch down among the folded rafts. He lowered the lid and began to wait.

13

The thirty-six hours that followed were some of the longest in Mack Bolan's life.

It was just after two o'clock on a Sunday afternoon when he first squeezed himself into the port side life raft locker. The *American Dream* didn't drop anchor again until after midnight on Monday.

There were nevertheless periods of intense activity during those thirty-six hours.

For the first forty minutes, Bolan heard nothing but hurried footsteps, shouted orders and occasionally, in the distance, a dispute between members of the squad detailed to check out the mysterious burst of machine-gun fire. Then there was a commotion on Promenade Deck, not far from the locker—excited voices, a heavy thump, somebody running.

Bolan raised the lid a fraction of an inch. After the total darkness of the closed locker, brilliant sunlight reflected off the deck momentarily dazzled him. Half closing his eyes to squint through the bar of brightness, he saw the loosened stateroom window leaning against the outer wall of the deckhouse. The man with the Mexican ring was leaning through the gap and gesticulating. "Belasko," he yelled, "the guy rooming with Mannering. The son of a bitch blew away Carlos. Had to be him. He's somewhere aboard. Find him."

Bolan lowered the lid as three men ran out from the shelter deck and headed for the rear of the ship.

"Engine room, stokers' and crew's quarters, cargo holds—especially the cargo holds. I want every corner of this goddamned tub turned over."

"And if we find the guy, do we shoot him, or what?"

"*When* you find him you bring him to the bridge. The boss wants him alive. He has questions to answer. If you have to shoot, and remember he's armed, shoot for the bastard's shins, knees, crotch. Nothing higher."

The footsteps receded, then rang on the steps of an iron ladder. "If necessary, you do a cabin-to-cabin search on every deck," the harsh voice called after them.

Some time later Bolan was aware that the ship was changing course. There was a slight swell now, and instead of rolling faintly the bow rose on the crest of each wave. He raised the lid a couple inches.

The deck was deserted. The shadows of the slung lifeboats, which had slanted diagonally across the promenade, had now swung outboard, and the deck was totally shadowed by the superstructure.

The *American Dream* had turned through ninety degrees and was shaping a course due west.

SOON AFTER NIGHTFALL, the distant drone of the helicopters shadowing the liner increased in volume. The pulse of approaching marine engines also percolated through the timbers of Bolan's locker. He heard a voice, distorted by a bullhorn, shout some kind of warning. Other loudspeakers, farther off, joined in. The sound of marine engines faded, but didn't entirely dwindle away. Then, from somewhere on the starboard side of the upper decks, came the tramp and shuffle of feet, a babble of high-pitched voices punctuated by curses and sharply spoken orders, the creak of rope and tackle.

Clearly there was some new development.

The bullhorn dialogue had warned that if the escorting flotilla came any closer, the terrorists would drop grenades among lifeboats, which they'd crammed with women and children and lowered on the starboard side of the vessel.

Where, the Executioner wondered, were the hostages headed now? Cuba? Jamaica? Nicaragua? Back to Panama or Colombia?

Whichever, it was going to be a long wait—especially if they stopped over at other places to pick up more arms.

More immediate, and more urgent, was the problem of Mannering. Once the commotion had died down and the ship was silent again, he decided to use the cover of darkness and check out the upper part of the ship. Mannering, he reckoned, would be held either on the bridge or in other quarters at that level, where the terrorist boss, who was directing the whole show, could get to him.

But first Bolan would check out **his** own level and the three passenger decks below. If he was to avoid guards and patrols, that could take most of the night. The guts of the ship, below C Deck, would have to wait.

He climbed warily out of the locker, stretched to ease his cramped limbs and padded along the darkened walkway below the lifeboats. He was less then halfway to the shelter deck when lights suddenly blazed to life, illuminating the entire port side of the liner with pitiless brilliance.

For a heartbeat, the Executioner was transfixed. He felt as exposed as a moth pinned to a display board.

He darted a glance right and left. No terrorists in sight...yet. It was too risky to try to make it back to the locker. He was carrying the Colt, but the rest of his weapons were in there and he might be seen raising the lid. So where?

One place only. He ducked under the nearest lifeboat, scrambled onto the rail, reached up until he could grab the rope loops fixing life belts to the craft's hull and hoisted himself until he was lying flat along the tarp stretched over the cockpit.

From there he could survey the length of the deck as well as the rear of the bridge wing and the officers' quarters without being seen himself.

A door opened at the forward end of the shelter deck, and the terrorist with the Mexican ring backed out. His SMG was pointed back inside the deckhouse. "All right you guys," he called in a voice less harsh than usual, "now that there are fewer of you, it's easier for us to keep you under control. So you get more freedom of movement. We're letting you take a walk, a dozen at a time, fifteen minutes for each group." He gestured with the gun barrel. "Okay. Come on out and take a lungful of that dandy ocean breeze!"

He stood off to one side, and a collection of men filed out, blinking in the bright light. Raising his head slightly, Bolan recognized several people.

"Toward the stern," the terrorist ordered. "And don't forget I'm right here with you. Any attempt to break away or act smart and I'll dust the whole damned dozen."

The twelve men moved off, staring around them at the lifeboats, the davits, the floodlighted superstructure and the dark sea beyond.

The hijacker brought up the rear, his weapon in the firing position. Bolan lowered his head as the group approached his hiding place—then swiftly raised it as pandemonium broke out above and behind them.

They swung around, the killer included. The noise came from the bridge. Through the windows in back of the wing, Bolan saw a knot of struggling, shouting figures—and in the center, unmistakable in his scarlet robe and striped pajama pants, there was Hillyard Mannering.

The passenger group stood rooted to the deck, as mesmerized as passersby hooked by a violent scene relayed on the multiple screens in the display window of a TV store. The guard made no move to hustle them away.

Mannering ducked and weaved, heaving his body desperately in an attempt to throw off the two men clinging to him and avoid the flailing fists of several others. Through the open window, Bolan could hear him shouting, but the words were lost in a volley of curses from the attackers.

Abruptly the struggle moved out of sight.

Feet pounded on an iron ladder. Something heavy fell, bumped, was dragged. The shouting rose to a crescendo on the Promenade Deck level, followed by a single, high-pitched cry.

And then, shockingly loud in the silence that followed, two shots from a heavy-caliber revolver rang out. A second later there was a third.

The passengers, who had watched the drama spellbound, now began talking animatedly among themselves. The man with the Mexican ring quelled the hubbub with a sharp command. "Shut up! Get going, all of you."

They turned obediently, then swung back to stare down the wide tunnel of the shelter deck. At the far end, where it opened onto the wide space below the bridge and above the cargo deck, there was movement.

Four guys in fatigues appeared beneath the floods. The leading pair dragged a fifth man by the heels—a limp figure with his head encased in an opaque plastic bag, a figure dressed in red-and-white striped pajama pants and a red silk robe emblazoned with black dragons.

Red smears, almost black in the fierce light, stained the deck as the group approached the rail.

The two terrorists bringing up the rear bent down and seized the dead man by the shoulders.

Then the four of them swung the body back and forth several times and heaved it over the side of the ship.

The garishly dressed corpse dropped out of sight, below the artificial illumination spreading from the foredeck and into the darkness of the ocean. The splash was lost in the churning of the liner's screws.

The Executioner was dumbfounded. He ground his teeth in rage and frustration, but there was nothing he could have done. No action he could have taken would have averted the drama. The suddenness, the unexpectedness of the shots, even after the struggle had started, would have preempted any suicidal rescue attempt he might have made.

He had no special feelings of warmth toward Mannering, but the Executioner and the West Pointer had been brothers-in-arms for a second time. Bolan had agreed to campaign with the man, and the warrior's loyalty was absolute.

He was angered by the brutality, the callousness, the uncalled-for violence of the terrorists' action. He was revolted by the whole ethos of the hostage-hijack scene. But more than anything else he was fired by the fidelity owed to a comrade in the fight. Mannering would be avenged.

The deck lights had been switched off once the passenger group had completed their fifteen-minute circuits of the Promenade Deck. Bolan dropped down from the lifeboat, made sure the coast was clear and hurried aft.

The locker lid was open. The stack of deck chairs had been moved and the exposed bloodstain gleamed dully in the starlight. Bolan didn't need to look inside the locker to know that the guns had gone.

"ON A TARGET the size of that ship," the Special Services colonel told Hal Brognola, "a commando-style raid could lead to a massacre. We don't know how many terrorists there are—and they're being smart, reducing their demands to a minimum, making no boasts, refusing to negotiate, failing to identify themselves. There's nothing for the military analysts to go on, not enough to help the voiceprint experts."

Brognola nodded tiredly. He hadn't slept for two nights, and his fleshy face was as crumpled as his suit. The roter whine of the Navy helicopter was giving him a headache, too. "If you knew who they were," he agreed, "or at least who they represented, you'd know the kind of people they were and therefore their probable reactions to any course of action you might take."

"You got it."

"And then you could base your tactics on the shrinks' evaluation?"

"Sure. It's not foolproof, but it's a hell of a lot better than working blind."

The colonel sighed, looking down through the chopper's Plexiglas blister at the wrinkled azure expanse of the Caribbean. The sun was rising behind them, and the bird's tiny shadow danced over the swell a long way ahead. Two corvettes were holding their position a couple miles behind and one mile north and south of the cruise ship. "You know how many places there are to hide on a ship like that?" the colonel asked, jerking his head at the streamlined black shape tipping the arrowhead of foam ahead. "To hide hostages, too. So, okay, we jump a squad onto the bridge and blow away the terrorists holding the officers and controlling the ship. Maybe we even rescue some hostages. Then some bastard says, 'We got fifteen more in the engine room, or the sail locker, or the crew's mess hall, and we're going to kill them one by one until you leave the liner.' What are we going to do then? Or when the *second* bunch comes out from under their stone and threatens to blow up fifteen more?"

Now it was Brognola's turn to sigh. "You tell me." It wasn't the cleverest rejoinder he'd ever come up with, but he was out on his feet.

The colonel went on, "Guy on one of those corvettes told me—well, he didn't exactly tell me, but we patched into a radio report before takeoff—he said one of the watchmen aboard, fellow who monitors the liner from dusk to dawn through night-vision equipment, saw some kind of commotion last night. He saw a crowd of people on the Promenade Deck, and *thinks* he saw a body thrown overboard. They made a couple of circles, sweeping the sea with searchlights, but nothing showed. The guy with the equipment said he had no idea who it was, passenger or hijacker.''

''I hope to hell that I know who it wasn't,'' Brognola said fervently.

14

Bolan was running.

They knew he was on the ship, had always known he was on the ship in the sense that they had a passenger list, that they were aware a man named Belasko shared a two-cabin stateroom with a man named Mannering. What they hadn't known until tonight was that Belasko was no ordinary passenger.

Belasko was a danger.

The Executioner had no way of knowing how much Mannering had given away, how much they had leaned on him before he was shot. Maybe, once they were wise to his SAFE connection, they had just assumed any companion of his must be a fighter and an enemy.

Maybe he hadn't spilled the secret of the life raft locker. He couldn't in any case have known Bolan was hiding in there.

But one thing was certain. Once they did discover the secret they'd know for sure that a guy who could leave an SMG and two powerful large-caliber automatics in his hiding place would be someone to watch out for. And someone, if he was on the loose, who would have a weapon on him.

A sudden thought crossed his mind. Would they assume he was still on board? Seeing that one of the rafts was missing, might they think that Belasko had taken his chance and gone over the side?

Negative.

If he had left the ship, he would have taken the guns with him.

It didn't take long for the terrorists to find the locker—it was open when Bolan returned immediately after the shooting.

The warrior had raced back up the Promenade Deck the moment he saw the open locker and, after a careful look inside, climbed through the dismantled window into the stateroom. He would have to find some kind of deep cover until the ship dropped anchor again, and then think of a way to get to shore.

Before that action, he would grab whatever he could in the way of evidence to pass on to the SAFE organization once he was free. In practice that meant the file cards stolen from the police HQ in Caracas, and Mannering's lists of contacts and connections in Brazil, Haiti and Panama. They were, Bolan knew, in the lining of the seersucker jacket Mannering had worn. Working quietly and as quickly as he could in the dark, he felt his way to the man's clothes closet and went through the garments hanging inside.

The seersucker jacket was there, all right, but the lining had been ripped away, and the papers and cards had been taken—as had Mannering's passport, driving license, SAFE credentials and the other papers he carried. The wallet he kept them in was lying open on a bureau at one side of the window. A billfold next to it was still stuffed with dollars, pesos and French francs, and plastic in place in its narrow pockets.

Bolan's brow furrowed. Why would the hijackers take the ID and leave the money? And they must have made a special journey to collect it because the guy had only been wearing pajamas when they took him.

"Yeah, Belasko," a voice said quite close to him. Bolan froze—then realized it was outside the open window. "He might try to make it back into this cabin. Ignazio, hide by that locker, where the bastard was yesterday. If he shows, let him go in, then corner him and call me. He'll be armed, but not with an SMG, so shoot if you have to, but not to kill, okay? Castaldo will be on guard in the passageway outside."

A second voice mumbled something Bolan couldn't make out.

"Shit, I *know* we already turned the whole fucking ship over. But while we're moving around, he can be, too. We can poke into some corner Belasko left ten minutes ago while he slips into an empty cabin we just finished searching. We have to keep at it, over and over, until we flush the bastard. And that's the boss's orders."

Bolan was at the cabin door. Was Castaldo already posted outside, or was he on his way, one of the voices outside the window? He tried the handle of the door. It turned soundlessly.

The big man peered into the corridor. There was no guard outside the door. He opened it wider. A terrorist stood at the far end, where a companionway led down to A Deck. His back was to the Executioner.

Bolan sped silently toward him. The man was holding an SMG, but the Colt remained in Bolan's shoulder rig. The sounds of a scuffle wouldn't carry as far as the discharge of the submachine gun.

But they could last longer. So speed was the name of the game.

The terrorist's MP-5 had no sling, so he was holding it loosely by the pistol grip, at arm's length.

Bolan leaped. In midair he raised his right foot and stamped it hard down on the stuttergun's retracted buttstock.

Torn out of the gunner's grasp by the unexpected blow, the SMG dropped to the floor. There was a clatter all right.

The terrorist swung around with a snarl of surprise. He was a big man, about Bolan's height and probably fifteen or twenty pounds heavier. Beneath the shortest possible boot camp crew cut, small eyes and a mean mouth bracketed a boxer's broken nose.

Bolan was still moving. Surprise, added to blurred vision from tears in the eyes, was a good beginning. The edge of his right hand, as hard and rigid as a nightstick, snapped into the cartilage between the guy's nostrils with the force of a jackhammer. Blood spurted from his nose, and he fell back a couple paces.

The Executioner stepped in and laid a straight left on the guard's nose and followed immediately with a right hook driven to the jaw. The guy went down, but didn't stay there. He'd fallen for one sucker punch and weathered two good ones to the face, but he bounced up like a rubber ball, swung a long, looping right to Bolan's own jaw and knocked him to the floor.

The warrior rammed the heels of both hands under the guy's chin to drive back his bloodied head, and rolled out from under. Springing to his feet, he kicked the gun out of reach.

The guard ran at him again, trading punches. Bolan moved in under a roundhouse left and hit the man hard in the stomach, twice, ducked back and jabbed him twice on his bleeding nose.

The Executioner took a heavy blow on the cheek-bone that rocked his head sideways, but the terrorist was already gasping for breath. Bolan threw one more punch, and the guy was suddenly sagging on rubber legs. It only took one more blow to finish him.

For an instant the terrorist teetered at the top of the companionway, then he crashed backward, falling down the steps in a tumble of arms and legs to lie on the floor of the passage below with his head at an unnatural angle.

Bolan, grabbing the fallen SMG, raced after him three steps at time. He leaped over the body and dashed past a row of cabins to an open space where there was a purser's office with doors opening onto a bar at one side and a barbershop on the other. Hijackers were shouting on the deck above, alerted by the noise.

Bolan was looking for a door marked Crew Only or No Entry. He found one behind the deserted American Bar. He slipped through the door and leaned his back against it, panting. He could hear feet now on the companionway.

A passage ran right and left behind the bar. Ten yards to his left he could see a hatch with a ladder leading below. He climbed down, keeping the Heckler & Koch well clear of the metal frame.

The crew's quarters on B Deck were very different from the ornate and extravagant section of the ship reserved for paying customers. They weren't squalid, and there was plenty of space, but bulkheads were steel instead of decorated wood; the furniture was simple, solid and functional with polished brass fittings; the layout everywhere put efficiency before style.

Only the human element was missing. Perhaps because the steady thrum of the turbines was louder down here, it seemed as if the ship was forging her way through the ocean alone, the wheel spinning as the swell determined, the rotation of the crews controlled by machines rather than men. But in reality nearly fifty crewmen and women had to be held somewhere at gunpoint. Male passengers were still locked into fifty of the cabins. The minimum number of hands necessary to run the ship—all of them presumably under guard— would be working the engine room, the galleys and the wheelhouse. And the officers were either confined to their cabins or forced to give navigational advice in the chart room.

On C Deck the broad companionway that took him below for the third time led to an anteroom outside the ballroom. Through an archway he looked across the huge floor at a ring of tables surrounding the dance floor with unfinished drinks collecting dust. Farther away he saw an unmade bed through an open cabin door, and then the copper and stainless steel desert of the main kitchens. He was reminded of a town from which the inhabitants had fled before an advancing army.

He crossed the kitchens, passed through stores and stopped at the entrance to a mess hall. He saw nobody, heard no footsteps, no voices, no click of a closing door. Only the tinkle of glassware on the long table broke the silence.

The vibration of the hull was pronounced here; the mess hall had to be directly over the engine room. Bolan turned the other way and took a long passage that led past locked doors toward the bows.

He wanted to familiarize himself with the terrain down here, but his aim was the nerve center of the liner—he wanted to be where the officers were held, in the area of the bridge, chart room and wheelhouse, where the terrorist chiefs made their decisions.

Inevitably this would involve taking big risks.

Risks, especially those where the odds were stacked against him, formed a major part of the Executioner's life-style.

Before he started to face them this time, however, he needed to complete his recon of this deck and the lowest levels below. More importantly he wanted to explore the cargo holds and examine the crates the hijackers had taken aboard each time the ship made port.

The long corridor turned through a right angle at the far end. He figured it would parallel the watertight bulkhead separating the holds from the passenger accommodation, and then run back aft on the far side of the vessel. And maybe, amidships, there would be doors giving access to the cargo space.

It did. But there weren't.

But there had to be some way through for the guys loading, stowing and unloading, and for the deckhands who wanted through into the fo'c'sle quarters. There was a hatchway and a ladder amidships. Bolan descended, and found himself in an area that was insufferably hot, and the thumping of the turbines uncomfortably loud.

There were doors in the bulkhead at that level, which were bolted, barred, shackled and controlled by a small wheel at each side like the strongroom doors of a bank vault—doors that were totally impervious to lock picks and any firepower from a 10 mm Colt or a Heckler & Koch submachine gun.

More vulnerable was Bolan himself. An identical SMG was lined up on him from fifty feet away, held by a thin-faced man in combat fatigues who had stepped through a door, halfway along the passage.

The warrior never knew what prompted the hair-trigger reaction that hurled him sideways at the instant he turned his head and saw the guy—the faintest noise, a barely audible rasp of cloth against metal, a tiny current of warm air displaced by the gunman's arrival?

A leaden deathstream flattened against the steel bulkhead as the narrow aisle echoed with the sounds of gunfire.

Bolan was on one knee, his own MP-5 spitting flame.

The hijacker pulled back into the doorway, out of range.

Bolan scrambled up and raced after him. He could have escaped around the corner of the passage, but he reckoned it would be prudent to take care of this threat first.

The corridor that led to the engine-room stairway linked Bolan's corridor and it's mirror image on the other side of the ship. In the middle was a steel sandbox with extinguishers and firefighting tools clipped to the wall above. The terrorist was hunched down behind the sandbox, and he opened fire as Bolan dived to the deck, slid forward and pumped out three shots from the Colt over the doorsill.

The sill was four inches high. The hijacker loosed two 3-round bursts, low, all of them blocked by the metal ledge.

Bolan was in a better position. He'd noted that the first long burst drilled into the bulkhead at knee height. Clearly the gunman was obeying the orders Bolan had heard—take him alive; shoot, but keep it below the waist.

Not an easy task when all you could see behind a metal barrier was the top of the man's head.

Sighting carefully, Bolan fired two shots from the Colt at the nozzle of the red fire extinguisher fixed to the wall above the sandbox. The nozzle disintegrated.

White foam boiled out and cascaded onto the gunman.

He jerked half upright, sputtering, arms flailing as the remorseless asphyxiating tide surged around and over him.

Bolan leveled the H&K and squeezed off a burst that stilled the struggling terrorist. He leaped over the body and ran for the companionway that led up to C Deck.

Someone down at engine-room level shouted, "Hey, Waldo! What the hell's going on?"

A gunshot whistled past the Executioner's ear when he was halfway up the steps.

He whirled around and spotted another hijacker, lining up a heavy six-shooter. Bolan's SMG belched flame, emptying the magazine. Sparks flew from the steel bulkhead as the terrorist ducked back out of sight. Bolan dropped the weapon and hurried to the top.

The holds, the packing cases, the final exploration of the lowest parts of the liner would all have to wait. The hounds were suddenly on his heels.

THE WARDROOM WAS all cream paint, polished mahogany and mirror-bright brass. The floor was narrow stripped-pine boards, preserved beneath a synthetic nonskid varnish. Bolan lay with one cheek pressed to the floor, concealed beneath a settee clamped to the bulkhead and covered by a polyamide material resembling chintz.

Bridge, chart room and wheelhouse weren't very far forward, each housing ship's officers and the terrorists who menaced them. But the radio operator's cabin was in between, and the cacophony of bleeps, call signs and static emerging from its unmanned console effectively drowned any conversations the Executioner might have overheard.

It was late afternoon on a Monday. The liner had left Martinique at midday, Sunday. The thirty hours at full-speed ahead, allowing for the change of course, Bolan figured they should have traveled between 550 and 600 miles. Where were they heading?

Puerto Rico was out; they had already bypassed it. The Central American isthmus was still more than 800 miles distant—too far perhaps, because the ship hadn't refueled since the takeover and had been traveling at maximum speed ever since.

Everything depended, therefore, on the next change of course. To port could mean a return to Colombia; a starboard course would imply Hispaniola—Haiti and the Dominican Republic—or maybe even Jamaica.

It had taken him several hours to reach his present hiding place—several hours of ducking and dodging among the deserted companionways and public rooms of the ship; of racing for cover in the warren of inter-connected spaces honeycombing the liner's hull, working his way ever upward to thwart the terrorists combing every corner of each deck.

The warrior's main aim at this point was to lay low until he could get off the ship and pass on to the SAFE officials the documents that he had in his possession.

Terrorists passed the wardroom several times, but nobody came inside. The turbines continued their even throb; the clatter of the chopper's rotors remained in the distance; the sunlight paled.

Soon now, Bolan thought. He had to wait for darkness to fall before he could become mobile again. There were still voices in the chart room; he wanted to hear what they were saying.

He emerged warily from beneath the settee when the liner heeled very slightly to port. The stars swung past the portholes from right to left. They were changing course, quite suddenly, onto a bearing that had to be almost due north.

Haiti?

Bolan figured some of the terrorists would soon make a round of the cabins that were still occupied. It was then, when the numbers on the bridge would be at their lowest, that it would be safest to act.

He guessed right. At nine o'clock four men—one for each deck, it seemed—left the bridge, climbed down the ladder to the Promenade Deck and separated. The normal two-man patrols, Bolan knew, had already been coopted for the search party, whose activities from time to time he heard faintly in the distance.

The Executioner crossed the dark wardroom to the door that led to the deck, and listened. He heard same murmur of voices, the same turbine throb, the same helicopter. Nothing nearer.

He opened the door, and saw that the deck between the bridge and the ladder was deserted. Aft of the streamlined smokestack, another ladder, much narrower and vertical, was clamped to the deckhouse wall. Flattening himself as much as he could, the warrior climbed to the deckhouse roof. He lay facedown, listened, then began inching forward in the direction of the bridge.

He was between two gooseneck ventilators when he heard a magnified voice.

"Striker, if you happen to be within earshot, listen to me..."

Bolan froze. It was unbelievable, but Hal Brognola was trying to get into contact with him.

Five feet in front of him, a glass skylight ventilating the radioman's cabin was open. The voice was coming from below this. One channel left open, one frequency tuned in, an amplifier turned up... It was possible.

It was for real. Brognola was talking.

"Listen, Striker...I'm in the chopper shadowing the ship. Can't say more. If you don't hear me, others will... But just in case, that one-in-a-thousand chance, I want to know if you're free, guy. If you are, give me some sort of signal..."

A door jerked open, and a man cursed. Bolan heard hurried footsteps.

"...any signal, a sheet hung out a porthole, a life belt thrown in the sea, anything out of the normal. We'll be watching. And if we see a sign we'll contact you somehow—"

The transmission ended abruptly. A man called out, "I *told* you to cut that fucking thing, Giorgio!"

"Shit, there's no harm done. So somebody broke in on an open channel. So what? And who the hell's Striker, anyway?"

"Search me. It has to be connected with Belasko. How come nobody has located the son of a bitch?"

"Man, it's a big ship. You know that."

"I don't give a fuck how big the ship is. We don't have much time left, and he's got to be found before we drop anchor."

Bolan's throat constricted. He crawled forward as fast as he dared. The second voice, the more distant one, was familiar. But if he was right, it was even more surprising, even less believable than the sound of Brognola's.

He was right.

A shaft of light lanced skyward through a sliding glass panel in the wheelhouse roof. The panel had been pushed back so that it was open about eighteen inches.

Bolan inched around so that he could peer down into the lighted space below. He saw the ship's captain, the first officer and the chief engineer, haggard and unshaven, handcuffed to metal chairs screwed to the floor behind the chart table. He saw a helmsman standing behind the wheel and a bearded terrorist covering the four men with an MP-5. He saw another table, farther back, that was covered with papers, land maps and scribbled notes.

Three men sat around the table, engaged in earnest discussion. Bolan recognized the terrorist who had murdered the passenger in the ballroom and the man with the Mexican ring.

The third man, smoking a long cigar and wearing fatigues, like the others, was Hillyard Mannering.

15

Amazement and disbelief warred with the evidence before Bolan's eyes. A look-alike? No way. It was Mannering, all right—the posture, leaning slightly forward in the chair with the head tilted, the drawled voice, the movements of the hands were as conclusive—more so, perhaps—than the features.

Yet he had with his own eyes seen Mannering fighting with the terrorists, heard the shots, watched in anger as Mannering's body was thrown into the ocean.

Wait.

What *exactly* had he seen?

Through the open window in back of the bridge wing, he had seen Mannering fighting with the hijackers. Unmistakably it was Hillyard Mannering—he had seen his face, recognized his voice.

Above all he had recognized the striped pajama pants and the red robe.

Then the struggle had moved out of view. It had moved down the companionway to the Promenade Deck. A gun, probably a revolver, had been fired.

A few moments later four terrorists reappeared dragging Mannering's body.

Correction!

Bolan remembered that the head had been covered by a plastic bag.

But not out of any sense of decency, respect for the dead, or because the expression on the face was alarming. It was to hide the fact that the body wasn't Mannering's.

Not, therefore, unmistakably Mannering's, but mistakenly his.

What Bolan had seen was *a* body, dressed in striped pajama pants and a red robe, thrown into the ocean. Because Mannering had been seen wearing those garments a short time before, he'd made the natural assumption.

So had twelve other people.

He remembered the words of the man with the Mexican ring. "Now that there are fewer of you, it's easier for us to keep you under control... We're letting you take a walk, a dozen at a time..."

And out the passengers had come, witnesses of irreproachable integrity and blameless character, just in time to see the Mannering drama. Bolan recalled that the terrorist in charge had *not* moved them on until the scene had been played out. And none of the other passengers had been brought out subsequently for the promised promenade.

Conclusion: those twelve passengers, specially chosen, perhaps, for their respectability, had been brought out on deck with one specific purpose—to witness the "death" of Hillyard Mannering.

Second conclusion, obvious enough: the whole deal was a setup, an elaborate charade engineered so that the man could fake his own demise and then join the hijackers.

Corroboration? Yeah, several points.

Mannering had clearly put on those distinctive clothes—possibly had brought them for that purpose—because he knew he'd be dragged away that morning. Had there been time for him to strip, then dress a dead man in them while he'd been out of sight?

Plenty.

Bolan remembered that the body had left fresh bloodstains on the deck. Very convincing. So the shots had killed someone who'd been held as a sacrificial lamb until the drama could be staged. He remembered the missing cabin steward, Flanagan. He was about Mannering's build.

And he realized now that the puzzle of the stolen ID papers and the billfold that was left untouched made sense. The ID would have been placed on the dead steward's body—confirmation, along with what remained of the clothes, if ever it was picked up. The money would be left because the scenario would be that Mannering was carrying the papers with him when he was taken away, though a sharp investigator might wonder why the man took his ID to bed with him.

Two questions remained in the warrior's mind—the first was why did Bolan fit into the scheme of things, and the second was how?

There was no question as to why they wanted him at all costs—alive until they found out how much he knew, then dead for sure. He was the one witness who could contradict all the others.

But why did Mannering enlist his help in the first place, and what did the man have to do with the perfectly legitimate SAFE organization?

For answers, the warrior decided to focus on the discussion going on below the skylight.

"We can waste a few soldiers," Mannering was saying, "burn a few farms and . . . persuade a few growers to see things our way. But the real problem is getting the stuff out—from the producers to the dealers. I guess you're familiar with the problem, Felix, from the other side?''

The terrorist who had murdered the passenger in the ballroom nodded. He seemed to be the hijackers' leader. "Transport," he agreed. "Routes. Safe conduct and reliability of the outlets. Always the same fucking thing."

"Exactly. Whichever way we do it, the Medellín cartel is likely to block us. There's no safe way to the coast or the existing strips." Mannering tapped a map of Colombia. "Until now."

"What did you have in mind?" a new, slightly sibilant voice inquired.

The man with the Mexican ring hadn't opened his mouth. Bolan shifted his position slightly so that he could see farther into the wheelhouse. The questioner was sitting some way from the map table, with his chair tipped back against the wall. There was another surprise for the Executioner when he recognized him.

It was the middle-aged Vietnamese who had been sitting at Bolan's own table in the dining room, one of the passengers brought out on deck to witness Mannering's fake death. Or to check that the other eleven took in what they were supposed to?

He was a businessman, the dapper Asiatic had told them, import-export, with connections in Southern California, Texas and Florida.

What, Bolan asked himself, could the guy be dealing in? Arms? Or drugs? It depended on the relationship between Mannering and the men who had taken over the ship.

"It's this mine," Mannering explained. "In the Caliente—one of the mountains behind Medellín. It's a coal mine, of a sort. But the seams are so narrow, sometimes no more than twenty inches deep, and running at right angles to the mountainside, that they can't get men to work them. I mean, there isn't space enough for an adult, so the Colombians use nine- and ten-year-old kids. In some of the distressed areas, and believe me there are plenty, kids of that age are the only ones in a family who can find work.''

The Vietnamese grimaced, as if he had had a bad smell thrust under his nose, and flicked a speck of dust off the sleeve of his white sharkskin suit. ''How uncivilized,'' he said.

''They work the face on hands and knees,'' Mannering continued, ''and back out pulling the coal bag after them. The only light they have is a candle in a kind of lantern that they hold between their teeth. Sometimes the shafts slant down as far as two hundred feet, in a temperature around ninety with no ventilation.''

''That's the kind of shit we fight against in my country,'' Mexican Ring said. He spit. ''How much do the little bastards get paid?''

''They have to hack out one thousand pounds of coal each day, no overtime, no extra money if they work into the night. If they're lucky they make four, five U.S. dollars a day.''

''Jesus!''

''I'm telling you this,'' Mannering said, ''because I figured they'd be kind of eager to make more than that. I'm paying them ten dollars a day—no point spoiling the market—to go right on digging.''

''What?''

''At night, when the overseers have gone, they go back in there and tunnel. Fuck the coal. They go on burrowing until finally they hit fresh air again on the far side of the mountain. I already got three passages right through. Soon the place'll be honeycombed!"

"Okay," the terrorist chief said. "I'll bite. Why?"

Mannering grinned. "Like you say, Felix. Transport. Anytime we take it down the coast, the cartel is likely to jump us, right? But if we were to tunnel the stuff inland . . . at first, anyway?"

Felix whistled. "You're telling me . . . ?"

"There's an uninhabited valley on the far side of the mountain. The stream in that valley leads to the Nechi River, and if you follow that to the swamps around Margarito and the airfield at El Banco . . ."

Mexican Ring nodded. "And there are always freelance pilots ready to make a quick buck around there."

"The coca fields, most of them, are within easy reach of that mountain," Mannering said. "We have the kids take the stuff in, already packaged, at night. We have collectors waiting the far side, who ferry it downriver to the swamps. After that, it's just a matter of air freight."

"Not via Cuba?" Felix asked.

"Not Cuba. Since Castro executed those two generals who allowed the cartel to use military airfields as a staging post, Cuba's kind of a sensitive area for individuals in the cocaine business." Mannering laughed. "There are other islands, even nearer."

"Jamaica? Haiti?"

"Uh-uh. Jamaica's too dangerous. Haiti's unreliable. Try a little farther east, just over the border."

"Got it. And from there?"

"One of the cays south of Andros Island, in the Bahamas. After that it's a ferry to Florida, and our friend takes over." Mannering nodded toward the Vietnamese.

He tipped his chair forward and sat up straight. "Very good," he said in his high, lisping voice. "Is a complicated route, but you are probably right. It's safest from hijack that way."

"Safest from attacks by Ortiz, too. And safest from meddling narcotics agents," Mannering said. "And believe me, I know!"

On the deckhouse roof, Mack Bolan expelled his breath in a long sigh. Of course he knew! What better way to beat the antidrug authorities, and to laugh in their faces, than to direct a privately funded international body working in with them?

He saw the whole plan now. Like all good schemes, it was simple—once you knew how it worked.

SAFE was a regular, respectable do-good operation—it was just Mannering who was the rotten apple in the barrel. Far from gathering information to smash the drug barons' evil trade, he was going into business himself!

He was setting up his own distribution network in opposition to the cartel, and beating the hell out of the Colombians whenever he could in the process.

Looked at in this way, a lot of things made sense.

Two cartel packaging and distribution centers, one in Colombia, one in Martinique, had been temporarily put out of business. Mannering had worked out his own way of transporting the stuff to the United States with the minimum risk of cartel interference. He had a list of crooked cops who could be paid to smooth over any rough passages here and there.

And stateside—this was a hunch on Bolan's part, but it seemed a safe bet—he would be in partnership with the new Vietnamese mafia that was terrorizing the West

Coast and spoiling for a fight to the death with the Hispanics in Florida.

Mannering was sitting pretty.

And Mack Bolan, unknowingly, had helped him get there. He'd helped overthrow one corrupt body so that it could be replaced by a worse one.

Bolan seethed.

The situation could be, would be, reversed...the game wasn't over yet. But before he could consider reprisals, there were still things he wanted clear in his mind.

First, one of the clever points in the plot was that nobody could finger Mannering as the brains and boss of the new organization. Hillyard Mannering was dead, murdered in front of unimpeachable witnesses and his remains consigned to the ocean. The new boss could remain anonymous, using any identity he cared to assume, a shadowy figure about whom police and narcotics agents would know nothing whatsoever.

The cartel knew something, though. Bolan remembered the words of Raul Ortiz. When he held them at the farm in Martinique. "I know why you're here...and I know who you're with and why." Something like that. He'd supposed the words referred to SAFE. But maybe they didn't.

He remembered the ambush they had run into when they landed on the French island—and realized that Mannering had probably killed honest cops who followed them into the hills. Was it too much to assume that the leak, the tip off, had in fact come from Ortiz?

He remembered, too, the mysteries in and around Medellín. Rafael Mendoza, the old man with the mule, had said that Harvey Lee and his flashy companion had come from far away, where fuel was dug from the mountain. Clearly Brognola's agent had discovered the secret of the tunnels destined for Mannering's cocaine train and been killed because of it. But had he also been working undercover for the cartel at the time? Had *they* killed him because he was blown? Or because they wanted to hide the fact that they knew about the tunnels?

According to Mannering himself, all the witnesses—Mendoza, his friend Pedro Díaz, the trucker who staged the car accident—had been eliminated by Ortiz to keep them from talking. The killers could as well have been Mannering's men, for the same reason. Specifically, in either case, to stop them talking to Bolan.

He filed the puzzle away for later examination.

But it looked very much as if Ortiz and his masters knew more about Mannering and his activities than the man realized.

"What are we going to do about this Ortiz?" The Vietnamese's voice shook Bolan from his reverie.

"Ortiz is an executive," Mannering replied. "He's tough and he's important, but the guys who call the tune, the ones who really count in the cartel, just rest their butts in their expensive hill properties and make phone calls."

"I'd be happier if he was out of the way," Felix said.

"He will be. Let's just complete this deal first, okay?" Mannering sounded irritated. "We drop anchor at midnight, and there are still details we have to thrash out. Including the Belasko problem."

Bolan moved slowly away from the skylight. He had heard all he needed to know. Midnight was in less than two hours and there were problems of his own that had to be thrashed out.

He understood why Mannering had talked him into the trip in the first place—he wanted a hardman along who had no connection with the drug business; if he was strictly antidrug, so much the better—it strengthened his own SAFE image. He knew why it was vital that he should be silenced now, but what he didn't know was the precise relationship between Mannering and the hijackers. The guy must have known about the hijack plans from the start, but how they fitted in with his own conspiracy remained a secret.

Bolan didn't know, either, what the purpose of the hijack was.

It seemed no ransom demands had yet been made.

The only requests to trade against the hostages' lives had been to allow the ship to sail wherever the terrorists wanted, and to load those crates of merchandise.

The crates, Bolan was convinced, were the key. He'd have to find out what was in them before the liner dropped anchor at midnight.

Before that he had to contrive a signal that Brognola in his chopper would see. Just to show, as the Fed demanded, that he was not being held prisoner.

Both problems, he figured, could be solved in the forward part of the ship.

Letting himself warily down the ladder to the Promenade Deck, the Executioner stole toward the bow.

16

Bolan gained the foredeck without much trouble. The moment of maximum risk was right at the start—he couldn't go below again because of the search parties, so the only way was down a ladder that led from the foremost section of the Promenade Deck, immediately below the bridge.

The deck was in darkness, but there was a reflection from the greenish light in the wheelhouse above. A gate in the railing opened above the ladder, but Bolan preferred to hoist himself over rather than handle it. The gate frame was heavy ironwork; the hinges could be stiff; metal exposed to salt winds and sea spray could grate or squeak.

The lookout in the bow should be staring ahead. It was unlikely that he would notice the briefest of movements above the rail behind him, especially against the glare from the bridge interior. The helmsman would see him for sure, but Bolan aimed to ignore that. The man was a crew member. If he realized the man at the rail was no hijacker, he wasn't going to tip off the terrorist holding a gun on him.

The hunch paid off. There was no hue and cry.

Bolan swung himself onto the polished wood rail, then lowered himself to the ladder. He moved forward among ventilating cowls, winches and coils of rope until he made the hatch covers.

Between the two main loading bays was an inspection hatch that allowed crew members to check out the cargo stowage to confirm that nothing had shifted in rough weather.

Unlike the hatch covers that slid on rails across the open holds, this was a simple flap that lifted like an ordinary trapdoor. Bolan had no trouble raising it until it clicked into place against a security catch, insulated from the deck by rubber buffers.

Except that as he straightened to go down the ladder beneath, he stared into the muzzle of a submachine gun held by a terrorist who stepped out from behind a windlass just forward of the hatch.

Evidently the lookout on the prow was sharp.

For Bolan this wasn't just a matter of acting quickly, of powering out some annihilating maneuver one hundredth of a second before the other guy. It was a question of instantaneous reflex, with death as the answer if the organism read the signals incorrectly.

His bunched left fist jerked up with stunning impact, knocking the gun barrel aside. His right hand, open and plank stiff, swung across at the same time to paralyze the gunner's wrist so that his fingers couldn't tighten on the trigger. And then, as a recoil action, his forehead smashed into the terrorist's face, splitting the skin over the bridge of the nose and blinding the man temporarily with tears. The gunner staggered back, stumbling over a hawser snaking across the deck as Bolan closed in fast and whipped out a left that knocked the man backward over the windlass.

The warrior vaulted over while the core and the wheel that controlled it were still spinning. He snatched up a loop of rope and dropped it over the hijacker's head before he could scramble upright. The SMG had already skated away across the deck.

The man gagged, clawing at the hemp circle biting into his neck, but Bolan had spread his arms wide, tightening inexorably the running knot he had thrown.

The hijacker's feet thumped the floor, slipping on the blood that dripped from his nose. He aimed a couple of wild blows at the Executioner, but the world was fading before his eyes as the noose cut off his oxygen supply. He crumpled and sagged.

Bolan dropped the body through the hatch, then climbed down the ladder and lowered the trap over his head.

The ladder led to a kind of gallery, a walkway athwart the hull from which both holds could be surveyed. One was packed with refrigerator containers, the other with Spanish SEAT automobiles destined for Brazil. Twin ladders plunged to the floor, and below again to where the smaller 'tween-decks merchandise was stowed. Bolan went down; the crates should be stacked in this area.

It took him some time to locate them. He knew they would be on an upper layer, nearest to the hatches, but there was a big area to cover. Finally the open cases in which the hijackers themselves had been smuggled aboard led him to the right corner.

The crates were of different shapes and sizes, the smallest about five feet long, the largest eight or ten. But all of them were addressed to Gomes Pereira SA, c.i.f. San Cristobal, S.D.

The stowaways had left the jimmies used to pry open their own crates lying around. Bolan took one and started on the nearest Pereira case. The light in the holds was very dim, little more than a pilot in each corner behind a metal cage. He switched on his penlight, shoved the flattened iron lip of the tool beneath the lid and levered it up.

The contents were no great surprise. Kalashnikovs—the latest AKM model—rows of them, still in greased factory wrappings. He tried another crate. Waterproofed Heckler & Koch caseless assault rifles. The third was packed with Browning, Walther and Colt pistols.

How many crates were there? Dozens.

How much time did he have? How soon would the lookout be missed? Anytime if the terrorists on the bridge were used to seeing him in silhouette on the prow. It was possible that he also prowled the foredeck, but the Executioner reckoned it would be reckless to trade on it. The terrorist was still slumped on the walkway, his neck broken by the fall. He hurried up and concealed the body in the trunk of one of the SEAT sedans.

Back among the crates, Bolan opened another half dozen at random. He saw Uzis, grenade launchers, bazookas with rocket-propelled missiles and mortars. There were also cases crammed with ammunition—HEAT, air burst and armor-piercing missiles, grenades, boxes of Octogen plastic explosives and thousands of rounds for automatic pistols, rifles and submachine guns.

He had taken a Walther PPK automatic to add to his own reduced armory and was selecting ammunition for it when he made the discovery.

Shifting a carton of .45-caliber shells so that he could open a 9 mm package for the new gun, he felt his fingers touch wood. He frowned. He had thought the crate was deeper than that.

He drew back, checked the outside, plunged his arm in again.

The crate *was* deeper.

A couple more measurements confirmed his suspicion; the case had a false bottom. There was a space of four or five inches between the inside and the outside.

He checked out the others.

Every case he had opened was the same—each one contained a secret storage space of the same depth.

A long crate containing grenade launchers was the quickest to empty—because they were heavy and cumbersome there were fewer pieces to move. He played the penlight beam around the inside. There was no obvious way of removing the false bottom. It must have been built into the crate when the contents of the secret compartment were already in place.

He picked up the jimmy and drove the flattened end as forcefully as he could into the seamless plywood sheet. At the third attempt, the wood split. He shoved in the tool and pushed until a portion splintered away.

Reflected light glimmered up from a hundred different surfaces. He shone the beam through the gap and saw dozens of neat packages filled with a fine white crystalline powder.

Bolan didn't need to rip one open to know that this was no secret cargo of West Indian sugar.

If each case contained the same amount of refined cocaine, the total street value would run into many millions—perhaps billions—of dollars.

He shook his head. Mannering was clever. He was running a double, in this case maybe triple, bluff.

Using an antidrug crusade as cover, he was setting up a distribution network to rival the Medellín cartel's. And as cover for this first huge consignment he had engineered a blaze of publicity worldwide that concerned the hijack of an ocean liner and the smuggling of arms.

Bolan realized now that there would be no ransom demand. The hostages had been taken with a single aim in view—to allow the ship to collect and deliver the crates unmolested.

The ingenious factor was the use of arms. Illegal shipments destined for revolutionaries, guerrillas or so-called freedom fighters were customarily shipped in crates labeled machine tools or agricultural machinery. Here the story was that the smugglers had hijacked a ship to obtain the same result...but the arms themselves were a blind!

Remembering the Bay of Pigs and the Iran-Contra scandal, Mannering had gambled on the Administration's unwillingness to interfere with attempts to overthrow a Communist regime on the U.S. doorstep. And while everyone was tut-tutting about the hijack—but carefully looking the other way—some Central American guerrillas would probably get at least some of the arms. But this huge drug consignment would secretly have been landed in Florida.

For nationwide distribution by the Vietnamese mafia that was making such horrendous inroads in the American underworld?

Bolan thought so. The Medellín cartel worked with the Families of the Sicilian-American Mob. It was logical that Mannering, working against the Colombians, should ally himself with the Asians who worked against the Mob.

He had probably made contact in those last days of the Vietnam War—at the time of the rumors that Bolan still vaguely recalled but could not pinpoint.

He sat back on his heels. So what was he going to do about it?

There were two immediate priorities: one, make the signal that would alert Hal Brognola; two, decide—in principle only—on his course of action when the *American Dream* dropped anchor at midnight.

Where would that be?

Mannering had said east of Haiti, just over the border.

Haiti's eastern frontier separated the country from the Dominican Republic, the other half of the ancient island of Hispaniola. And, remembering the consignment instructions on the crates, Bolan recalled there *was* a small port named San Cristobal in the Republic. The "S.D." that followed could refer to Santo Domingo, the capital, which was nearby. Maybe the cruise liner was at the end of its unscheduled voyage.

Bolan looked at the waterproofed watch strapped to his wrist. Another twenty minutes.

He had no wish to help the cartel, but it seemed to him that his moral duty, first, was to hit Mannering hard. Especially since he had himself unknowingly helped... He put the thought from his mind. He would play it by ear, but once the boat docked, every fiber of his being would be concentrated on that hit.

He was aware suddenly of movement and noise above.

Light suddenly streamed into the upper holds as the hatch that led to the foredeck was flung open. Bolan heard voices.

"...supposed to spell the bastard at a quarter to twelve, but he never showed."

"But where could he be?"

"We've had nothing but trouble on this trip!"

"I guess we better check below."

Bolan heard feet on the iron ladder. There was no place for him to go but down. There was no time to replace the crate covers. Swiftly he piled the grenade launchers back into their box. At least that might conceal the fact that he had discovered the drugs.

The foredeck was floodlighted. Flashlight beams probed the spaces between containers and cars. Somebody above stumbled and cursed. Bolan crept forward as close to the hull plates as he could. Brognola's signal would have to wait. Right now the essential thing was to keep out of the terrorists' way.

A door in the forward bulkhead led to a storage area beneath the crew's quarters. Below this another ladder plunged to a space deep in the liner's stem where the chain locker was situated.

Bolan climbed in and crouched down behind the huge iron links of the coiled chain. A moment later, a distant shout told him that the missing lookout's body had been discovered.

17

Five minutes later, Bolan was forced to leave his hiding place.

The thrumming of the cruise ship's turbines changed abruptly to a deeper, louder note as the engine-room telegraph chimed to full-speed astern. And then, with a roar and a rattle, the chain bounded upward out of the locker. The liner was dropping anchor.

Bolan got out of there fast. It was possible that he could have lost an arm or leg when the giant links were uncoiling.

By the time the turbines were cut and the ship had lost way to rock gently on the swell, he was back in the storeroom. Prowling through the supplies, he found a small jerrican of kerosene in the hardware section. He took it with him and padded back to the merchandise hold, the Walther in his free hand.

He was gambling now. If they had dropped anchor, the ship should be relatively near the shore. If this was the hijackers' final destination, at least some of them had to be concentrating more on the disembarkation of the crates than on the search for him. And if he guessed right on those two points, he could as a last resort leap overboard and swim for it if the going got too rough.

Because from now on he was going to have to come out into the open.

First priority: the signal for Brognola.

In a corner of the hold diagonally across from the arms crates, he had noticed bales of lightweight Indian cotton stacked on a wooden platform loaded from a forklift truck. He pried away one of these and soaked it carefully in kerosene.

By the crates, he unloaded the grenade launchers for the second time, poured the rest of the jerrican's contents in among the packages of coke and reached for wax candles and matches he had found in the stores.

Voices from the main holds above filtered down past the ladders.

"We searched every goddamn one of those cars—inside, underneath, the trunks. Zero. What about the containers?"

"Use your head. They're sealed and refrigerated. He couldn't have."

"Then the bastard *has* to be below. Come on, let's go."

Boots rang on the ladders. Bolan picked out a couple grenades and a carton of 9 mm ammunition, dropped them into the open crate and added a fistful of packing straw.

"Christ," one of the searchers exclaimed, "there's one hell of a stink down here! Smells to me like kerosene."

Bolan lighted a candle, set fire to the straw and ran. He ducked behind the ladder as the terrorists came down, snatching up the cotton bale in passing.

"*Jesus!* There's flames over there!"

"If those missiles were to go off..."

The three men dropped from the ladder and rushed toward the fire.

Bolan dashed up the ladder.

The fire was a delaying tactic, no more. Heat would soon melt the wax sealing the automatic sprinkler system; there was firefighting equipment in each sector of every deck. The contents of one crate, therefore, would be destroyed but nothing more.

A sudden hissing signaled that the kerosene ignited. Flames shot toward the roof. "Isolate the bastard! Shift those goddamn crates!" the chief searcher yelled. He ran for an extinguisher and an ax, which was clamped to the bulkhead. The sprinklers in the roof started to spray water.

As Bolan shot through the hatch into the main hold above, he heard the firecracker volley of ammunition exploding, then a shout of unmistakable terror.

A rocket grenade tore through the iron decking that separated the two levels and burst with a shattering concussion beneath one of the SEAT sedans. The livid flash of the explosion was instantly eclipsed by a blazing fireball as the car's fuel tank erupted. Flames licked the vehicles on either side, and the hold filled with choking black smoke from burning tires.

This was better than Bolan had hoped for. He ran up the companionway to the gallery above. After that it was just a question of maneuvering the kerosene-soaked cotton bale through the trapdoor onto the foredeck.

But someone had seen him. There had been a fourth man in the main hold, who shouted through the smoke. An answering voice replied from below. Bolan heard three revolver shots. Bullets vibrated the iron stairway, flattening themselves against the treads. The cotton bale jerked as a slug buried itself in the material.

The warrior whirled around beneath the open trap and pumped two shots from the Walther into the flame-tinged smoke. Then he shoved the bale through the opening and scrambled after it onto the floodlighted foredeck.

Two more hijackers were running down from the bridge, a third from beneath the shelter deck. They hadn't seen the Executioner yet. He dodged behind a dinghy that was lashed upside down beyond the windlass.

The cracks between the main hatch covers and the deck were outlined in a pulsing crimson glare. "Don't slide back the hatches!" a voice from the bridge screamed. "The draft . . . You'll have the whole goddamn ship on fire!"

"What about the crew up for'ard?"

"Fuck the crew. They're behind fire doors anyway. Kill those flames and contain the fire down there." The terrorists vanished below.

Bolan was at the rail. He cocked his head, listening. The drone and clatter of a chopper was still audible somewhere astern. He glanced over the rail and took in the scene at a glance.

Humped, tree-covered hills against a starlit sky; lights from a small fishing port reflected in the dark water— it could have been Martinique again. The shore was perhaps half a mile away. Farther off, on the eastern side of a wide bay, a bright glare stained the dark over a larger town. Bolan guessed that must be Santo Domingo.

He lighted another candle, held the flame to the kerosene-soaked cotton, waited until much of the bale was ablaze, then seized the far end, heaved it up onto the rail and pushed it into the sea.

He leaned over, mentally crossing his fingers that the splash didn't extinguish all the flames.

No...some had been doused, but the bale was still burning fiercely. And the cloth, partly unrolled now, floated. As he watched, another section fired up, and the small island of flaming cloth drifted slowly past the ship's stern and out toward the open sea.

Brognola had to interpret that as a signal... In any case it was the best he could do.

Suddenly a pair of SMGs spit flickering death as two more men ran toward him from the deckhouse. A storm window on the bridge slid aside and a third man hammered out a deadly spray of 9 mm slugs. Bullets scored the deck, splintered the timbers of the dinghy and shrilled into the night.

Bolan backed up, firing the Walther, but there was only one place he could go. He stuffed the gun into his waistband, leaped over the side and dived into the ocean.

18

"Lucky, I guess," Hal Brognola said, "but I read that flaming bundle flung overboard as meaning the heat was on and you were taking to the water."

"That was more than I intended, but it worked out just fine."

He'd been halfway to the shore, with a launch lowered from the liner gaining fast, when the chopper's roving searchlight picked him up and he was able to grab a ladder lowered from the blister. The hijackers had opened fire, but the H&K submachine gun was beyond its effective range. And a target soaring skyward in the dark was difficult to hit.

Back at the base, aboard a carrier ten miles offshore, Bolan had briefed the big Fed on all he knew. It had taken more than an hour, with Brognola taking copious notes while Bolan attacked the first meal he'd had in countless hours. Now they were into the forward planning phase.

"One of the cays south of Andros Island, in the Bahamas," Brognola mused. "If that's the final destination before the Viets take over, we should be able to do something. It's two hundred miles from the Florida Keys, easy to keep under surveillance because the islands are flat. Maybe we could persuade the locals to row in help from the Brits in the Caicos."

"Could be." The Executioner was dubious. "But we only have one quote from one guy, overheard in tough conditions, telling us it *is* Andros. And they might drop off different consignments on the way. There's one hell of a lot of dope on that ship, even if the fire was a bonanza I hadn't counted on."

"It took them seventy minutes to control it."

"Okay, but they'd have shifted those crates first, I'm telling you."

"What do you suggest?"

"We hit the delivery right here, while it's still in one piece."

"Hell, Striker, we can't do that! This is a sovereign country, even if it is only a banana republic. You know how sensitive international relations are around here. Remember Grenada."

"I'm not saying we should send in the fleet," Bolan argued.

"What are you saying?"

"We can assume the Dominicans are being paid to look the other way. My guess is, the crates will be landed openly. They might even have end-user certificates for the arms right there. Or maybe they'll end up with the right wing rebels in Central America. Whatever, the cocaine's going to be separated from the arms as soon as the crates hit town."

"So?"

"So the coke's more important. To us, anyway. And I guess to the Administration. They should worry if the Contras or their friends next door win another bunch of missiles. But if one-tenth of that consignment's turned into crack, hell, half the population will be stoned forever."

"I read you, Striker. Hit the dope while it's in one piece, before it takes off on the first leg of the flight to Florida. Okay, okay. But how? Like I say, we can't risk sending in even the smallest—"

"You send in nobody." Bolan sighed. "Look, it's not just the coke. Mannering's whole network has to be wiped out. We can't bust the cartel, but we can bust him."

SAN CRISTOBAL WAS exactly what Mack Bolan would have expected of a small fishing port in a poor country in the Caribbean—tall shuttered houses with iron balconies fronting the quays; a waterfront market with bright fruits on sale beneath rattan shelters; sailboats, caïques, shabby fishing smacks and an occasional ritzy cruiser alongside a jetty; lobster traps and palm trees; clapboard shanties and white stone villas; shiny Cadillacs beside old Plymouths jacked up on bricks. The rich folks, those in with a dictatorial administration, lived on the high ground behind, above the smells.

Bolan aimed to mingle with the poor. Still unshaven, he wore frayed Levi's, no shoes and had a wide-brimmed straw hat pulled low over his forehead. A red flowered shirt hid a Beretta in a shoulder rig and a Desert Eagle in a hip holster, which the aircraft carrier's armory had supplied.

Risking international repercussions and an official UN complaint, the chopper had landed the Executioner on a deserted beach between San Cristobal and Nizao after an illegal flight through Dominican airspace. He had snatched a couple hours of much-needed sleep and then set off for the port on foot soon after dawn.

He kept to the dirt roads that paralleled the shore. The island's only expressway linked the capital with San Cristobal on one side and the international airport on the other.

As soon as he hit the outskirts of town, before the sun had showed above the waterfront roofs east of the harbor, Bolan knew this was no ordinary day. The *American Dream* still lay at anchor a half mile offshore. So far there was no sign of activity aboard. Two U.S. Navy corvettes were visible hull-down on the horizon; there was a chopper somewhere in the sky. But the tension in the air had nothing to do with any of that. The shantytowns hummed with activity. Snatches of calypso and reggae thumped and jangled from a hundred radios. The streets filled with people as he approached the center. There was a lot of laughing, then snatches of drunken song from the bars around the port.

It was only when he passed an alley that ran between a stained concrete apartment building and a rundown clapboard house that he caught on. At the far end of the alley, several black families were threading hibiscus, magnolia and strelizia flowers through a corded net that covered the rear half of an ancient flatbed truck.

An old ladder-back chair tied to the roof of the cab was twined around with tendrils of ivy, and there were sheaves of corn fixed over the fenders.

It finally clicked. Working forward from Sunday noon in Fort-de-France, Bolan arrived at Tuesday morning. Sure—but today was no ordinary Tuesday. It was Shrove Tuesday, Fat Tuesday, Mardi Gras. He remembered the liner's sailing schedule. They should have been anchored off Rio today for the annual carnival.

Well, San Cristobal was no Rio de Janeiro, but they were celebrating Mardi Gras with a carnival just the same.

By eight o'clock, crowds—many of them already costumed—jammed the streets around the port. The first parade, Bolan saw from a poster outside a bar, started three hours later. By nine, the jingle of wire stays against aluminum masts around the harbor was already drowned by the strains of at least three separate bands tuning up around the center.

The freshening breeze that agitated the stays and rocked the sailboats at their moorings was stirring whitecaps from the water outside the harbor. Bolan had found himself a perch on the seawall, along with several hundred other sightseers and tourists, from which he could watch equally well the cruise liner and the far side of the port, where the customs shed, a line of derricks and a launching ramp were located.

At a quarter to ten, officials and police wearing black shades cordoned off that part of the quay. Two patrol cars with flashing lights blocked the way for pedestrians. A lighter drew away from the jetty and chugged out toward the *American Dream*.

Bolan had no binoculars, but he could see that the derricks on the cruise ship's foredeck were swinging free. There were crates on the deck where a portion of rail had been removed. The distance was too great for him to make out grappling hooks, but the stack of crates nevertheless grew each time the derricks moved, and cargo was winched up from the holds.

By ten-fifteen the lighter was moored alongside and stevedores began stowing the crates as they were lowered from the liner. Bolan counted the crates—there were forty-seven in all.

The off-loading took a full hour. The lighter, riding low in the water now, plowed heavily through a choppy crosscurrent to tie up outside the customs shed at seventeen minutes short of eleven o'clock. A mobile crane on a gantry slid level with the shed's open doors and started to transfer the cargo ashore.

Other than the policemen blocking that end of the quay, Bolan could see no sign of official interest in the maneuver—the shipment could have been a regular freight delivery rather than a load of contraband taken off a hijacked liner that had made front-page news for nearly a week.

The doors of the shed closed at noon.

The crowd thronging the waterfront had grown increasingly noisy. White teeth flashed in dark faces. Teenage girls with linked arms giggled their way past groups of young men in bright shirts, and there was a burst of laughter and the sound of breaking glass from one of the waterfront bars. Many of the tourists wore paper hats.

Bolan saw that the market stalls had been closed up. From over the rooftops he could hear a babble of voices, the faint sound of musical instruments, clapping, cheering, the stamping of feet. Then, distant at first but rapidly approaching, came the syncopated throb of drums.

Excitement swept through the crowd—the first parade had to be heading toward the harbor.

Bolan began working his way around to the customs quay. Behind the closed doors of the shed, he was convinced, the crates had been upended and the bottoms levered off so that the packages of cocaine could be transferred in a single huge consignment. He was fairly sure that some of the hijackers, no longer wearing their fatigues, had come ashore with the crew of the small barge.

It was tough shouldering through the press. Bolan was additionally impeded by a satchel on a strap in which he carried half a bottle of wine, a loaf of bread and some fruit. Two pounds of plastic explosives and a detonator were secreted beneath the food.

He had almost made it to the landward end of the customs quay when there was a sudden shrilling of police whistles. A squad of uniformed men jumped down from an open-sided vehicle and began shoving back the crowd, forcing open a lane to the customs house. The crowd protested; some of the people were losing vantage points that they'd occupied since dawn. But gradually a way was cleared, and a canvas-topped truck backed up and disappeared into the shed. During the temporary lull, Bolan heard the unmistakable rattle of automatic gunfire across the water.

He jumped onto an iron hitching post and stared out over the breakwater. He spotted half a dozen men boarding a small launch. When the boat pulled away, Bolan realized to his surprise that the *American Dream* was weighing anchor.

As he watched, the ship turned and headed out to sea.

Bolan wondered what the hell was going on. Could the cargo that was off-loaded be completely different? Have nothing to do with the arms and the cocaine?

No way. Hell, he had recognized the crates. And surely the launch had to be bringing the last of the terrorists ashore! So what did the gunshots mean, and why was the ship sailing away?

Those questions had to wait. There were more pressing problems to solve. The truck had reappeared, the canvas flaps over the tailgate laced together. It was clearly going to turn away from the crowd, clear of the packed port, and he was on the wrong side of the lane.

He tried to jump the police line cross the lane, but two burly policemen barred his way. "Look," he began, "I have to get—"

"What's important is what we tell you, buster," the tougher cop said. He shoved the barrel of a mini-Uzi against the Executioner's chest. "Now get back there unless you want trouble."

For the moment Bolan allowed himself to be bested. The last thing he could afford was a run-in with the local law. By the time the police broke up the line and left, the truck was a block away, forging steadily through the mass of humanity streaming toward the waterfront.

It was moving slowly, but still way ahead of a guy trying to force his way against the tide on foot.

After ten minutes, he gave up on the chase, cursing. He had hoped to follow the drug cargo to whatever airstrip Mannering had selected for the next stage of the journey. He had hoped to rent a car so that he could follow easily and anonymously. Even when he discovered the rental agencies were closed because of Mardi Gras, he had hoped the crowds would be dense enough for him to keep up on foot. But he hadn't reckoned on the police clearing a way for that truck.

He climbed to the top of the breakwater and scanned the ocean. The cruise liner was about four or five miles away. A helicopter hovered over the stern, and the two Navy corvettes were closing in. Nearer inshore, the launch was approaching the harbor mouth. Bolan could recognize Mannering, Felix, the man he thought of as Mexican Ring, and two other terrorists.

At the last moment the boat swung wide, leaving a foamy wake as it changed direction and arrowed toward a small beach on the far side of the port. Bolan jumped to the ground and began to run.

If he couldn't follow the illicit cargo itself, he could at least tail the guy who would surely join up with it later—if he could make that beach before the launch ran aground and the terrorists landed.

He couldn't. There were too many stalls, too many parked cars, too much fishing gear on the quayside, and above all too many revelers jokingly trying to bar his route. But he made a low bluff overlooking the shore in time to see that the launch wasn't beached.

Mannering, Felix and Mexican Ring jumped out in the shallows and splashed ashore while the boat backed off, turned, and made for the port. Perhaps the remaining terrorists were due in the customs shed to handle the formalities relating to the weapons.

That aspect of the equation didn't interest the Executioner. The drug consignment and the men handling it were his target.

They climbed a sandy path from the beach. Bolan could go no closer. There was no cover between them. The three men stopped in the middle of a dirt road that followed the shoreline. Bolan was flat on his stomach among long grasses blowing in the wind.

"Okay, guys," he heard Mannering say. "You know where to go. RDV at six. I have to make it into town to check with the pilot."

Felix and Mexican Ring nodded. They set off westward along the dirt road, away from the port. Mannering headed in the other direction.

Bolan frowned. Whom should he tail? It seemed like the two terrorists were to go directly to the strip, but the meet was several hours away. What would they be doing in between? Drinking? Visiting buddies or relatives on the island? He had no idea, but he was convinced the rendezvous had to be much nearer the town than a several hour walk. He figured it was a better bet to stay close to the boss. Sauntering along the top of the bluff, his head turned mainly toward the ocean, he paralleled Mannering's brisk walk along the dirt road until he reached town.

After that, things became tougher.

The carnival was now in full swing across the waterfront area. The square behind the port, every side street and alley, was crammed with dancers weaving and bouncing to the music of three different bands. Guitars, mandolins, accordions, flutes, an occasional horn—and everywhere among them was the insistent pounding of percussion: hand-beaten conga drums, timbales thrashed with sticks, tom-toms, maracas, guiros and above all bongos, fingered and slapped by amateurs and professionals, bandsmen and individuals in a complexity of rhythms that galvanized the crowd.

As Mannering strode in among the surging mass of dancers, a parade appeared bright with huge papier-mâché masks and jumbo-size balloons in the shape of mythical animals. Floats carrying effigies strewn with flowers spearheaded a line of thirty-foot monsters, garish with colored paper, floating in the air from wires.

The noise was deafening. The air was full of confetti and paper streamers. Spun around by a sudden rush of costumed dancers, Bolan was just in time to see Mannering take delivery of a headdress from a stall selling favors and carnival masks. It was an elaborate affair, an outsized Chinese coolie head with Oriental features topped by a three-tiered pagoda hat. From inside, Mannering could look out through the eyeholes and check whether he was being followed without being recognized himself.

The man was taking precautions. But wearing carnival masks was a game two could play. The Executioner pushed his way to the stall and bought one himself—the head and neck of a beaked bird with feathers that cascaded almost to the ground. Looking out through the bird's large round eyes, he carried the straw hat he had been wearing in one hand and set off in pursuit of Mannering.

The pagoda hat was fifty yards away, near a flatbed truck transporting half a dozen bare-breasted girls garlanded with leis of white flowers.

The drums thudded on either side. Isolated snatches of conversation broke the complex surface of carnival sound like bubbles in a glass of champagne.

"He used to be a drummer with the Mango Boys, but now..."

"Hey, Charlie! Over here for God's sake!"

"...perhaps, later. There's a barman at the Fresco. You dig?"

"Room for a little one on that muscular arm, handsome?"

The coolie head was moving fast. Bobbing now near, now far away, it was clear that Mannering was heading for the fringes of the crowd. Bolan shouldered merrymakers aside, trying to close the distance between them. "What's your hurry, honey?" a fat women in a jockey cap laughed. A girl twined an arm through the feathers and around Bolan's neck, kissing the outside of the mask. Several times the Executioner risked being separated from his quarry by lines of singing dancers whose arms were linked. Once he did lose sight of Mannering altogether when a circle of howling admirers surrounded an amazon in tight blue jeans who decided to give a frenzied exhibition of acrobatics. Then he homed in on the coolie face once more, farther to the left than he expected, hurrying up a side street away from the waterfront.

Bolan vectored in, keeping his distance. Mannering crossed two busy avenues and climbed a flight of steps toward the higher ground in back of the old town. On all sides the yowl of electric guitars and the rattle of tambourines filled the air. The stairway was disgorging from the houses on either side a stream of plastic Popeyes, dragons and Disney characters, all pressing toward the port.

The pagoda hat traversed a cobbled square and stopped by a line of parked cars below a wooded hillside dotted with cabins among the trees. More than once Bolan had been forced to dodge into a doorway or crouch behind a car when the grotesque head turned to look behind.

Mannering stopped beside a gray Mercedes sedan, raised his arms and lifted the coolie head from his shoulders.

Only it wasn't Mannering.

The Executioner stared disbelievingly at the bearded features of Raul Ortiz.

19

His disbelief was momentary. The vendors of carnival masks would sell more than one of the same model. Bolan had followed one Chinese coolie head, lost it and picked up another in error.

But Ortiz? What was he doing in San Cristobal? How did he get there? How did he know?

A single fact could answer all the questions. The Executioner remembered again that Mannering had spoken of a leak.

Ortiz was in town because he knew of the cocaine shipment. No other explanation made any sense. There were a dozen ways he could have made it to the Dominican Republic, once he knew the hijacked liner was heading there. And he knew because of the leak.

If he knew that much, Bolan reasoned, if his intel was that good, he had to also know of the next stage in the operation. Otherwise why was he here at all?

In which case following Ortiz should lead him to Mannering's rendezvous. From where Bolan stood, no other option was open to him.

Where he stood was in a vandalized telephone booth. Nobody local was going to try to use the phone. But Ortiz wasn't local. He'd see nothing unusual in a guy apparently making a call from a pay phone.

Providing the guy didn't stay there too long.

Bolan glanced across the street. The Colombian had opened the trunk of the Mercedes. He threw in the Chinese mask and closed the lid. He was looking up the hillside toward the cabins among the trees.

Maybe he'd noticed the beaked bird, making his way here from the port. Bolan eased off his own headdress and allowed it to drop to the stained floor of the phone booth. He placed the straw hat on his head, maneuvered the Beretta from beneath his shirt and chambered a round.

Ortiz was looking up and down the street, and his gaze swept incuriously over the man in the straw hat making a phone call. He turned and began climbing a path that led to one of the cabins.

Bolan took the damaged handset away from his ear and holstered the Beretta. He left the phone booth and crossed the street.

In his turn, he took in the scene. The sidewalks were deserted. The two- and three-storied houses opposite the hillside had few windows facing the roadway; their balconies looked toward the ocean. The Mercedes was parked beneath the branches of a large magnolia, hidden from most of the cabins.

Bolan stood beside the vehicle. Was he right, believing Ortiz had closed the trunk without locking it? He pressed the catch and the lid sprang open.

From now on, success or failure depended on a hunch.

The Executioner backed his hunches. For what in fact was a hunch? It was the brain as computer, the simultaneous retrieval and evaluation of data gained over many years of skilled experience, balanced against a current input of unquantifiable impressions and resulting in a printout quicker than conscious thought.

Bolan's hunch was that Ortiz wouldn't have an automobile in San Cristobal unless he intended to use it for a very specific purpose...and that this purpose had to be a journey to the landing strip where Mannering intended to load his cocaine onto an airplane.

If the Colombian was on his way there, Bolan was on his way, too.

He checked out the catch on the trunk lid. The design didn't allow for it to be opened from the inside. Why would it? But the hooked steel arm that secured the catch could be pressed back against a strong spring by something hard and metallic, such as a gun barrel.

Bolan climbed into the trunk and pulled the lid shut after him.

The trunk smelled of leather upholstery and rubber and the tarry backing to the carpet, spiced with a tang of fresh paint from the coolie headdress. Bolan looked at the luminous dial of his watch. It was fifteen minutes short of four o'clock.

Mannering's RDV was at six. The time it took Ortiz to drive there would give him a rough idea of the distance involved. Bolan unleathered the Beretta, made himself as comfortable as he could in the confined space and prepared to wait.

HE WAITED until five-thirty, when he heard footsteps then growling masculine voices that nevertheless spoke with the liquid intonation of South American Spanish. Bolan tensed, the Beretta cocked in his right hand, ready to leap out shooting if the trunk was opened. But the lid remained closed. Anything Ortiz and his friends carried, they preferred to keep with them.

He figured there were five, counting the Colombian himself. The Mercedes rocked on its springs, settled a fraction lower as the doors opened, closed and the men sank into the seats. The engine was started and the sedan moved off.

For ten minutes they climbed, then the road flattened out but the surface became rough and eventually twisty. As far as Bolan was able to tell, from the incomplete count of grades and curves that he made, Ortiz had driven inland, wound up into the foothills, then taken a mountain road that crossed some kind of plateau northeast of the port. They must have covered about ten or twelve miles.

He heard only one exchange during the whole trip.

A voice he didn't recognize said, "Do we waste the bastards right away?"

"Hell, no." This was Ortiz. "There's talking to do first."

"What about the pilot?" a third man asked.

"The pilot's strictly untouchable and don't forget it. He has to be . . . persuaded to work for us. At least this once. We can get rid of him later, when the job's done. Paco says the ship's big enough for all of us, as well as the shit."

"So long as the mother's fit to fly," another man said somberly.

A few minutes later, the Mercedes bumped to a halt and the engine was cut. Doors opened, and the sedan rocked again as the drug dealers got out. Bolan heard footsteps—careful, quiet footsteps, crunching warily over stony ground. Ortiz said, "Okay, you know your places. We wait until Mannering's flyboy arrives, give him two or three minutes, then bust in." Seconds later, from farther away he added, "Shit, I almost forgot! Ruiz, there's one of those carnival masks in the trunk. It's the same as the one Mannering was toting. Maybe we could deal the soldiers an extra surprise if they think they see *two* Mannerings. You better go get it.''

The footsteps faded, all except one set, which grew louder as Ruiz approached the car. Bolan tensed. He reached for the satchel he still had with him and drew out the half-filled wine bottle.

The footsteps stopped, and the catch of the trunk snicked back.

The lid popped open, and at the same time Bolan sprang up, the bottle grasped by the neck, and smashed a vicious blow against the side of Ruiz's head.

The man was taken completely by surprise. He staggered back, hands flying up involuntarily to protect his face. Before he could yell, Bolan butted him fiercely on the bridge of the nose and closed viselike fingers around his neck. The bottle smashed on the ground.

After the first shock, Ruiz reacted fast. He was about Bolan's build, quick on his feet and tough. He hammered back at once. But for the Executioner this was a close encounter of a very special kind—there couldn't be a gunshot, no scuffling sounds of a struggle, above all no shout or cry. Which meant that, whatever happened, he had to keep his grip on the guy's throat.

With the impetus of his original leap, the Executioner dragged Ruiz to the ground, thumbs boring into his windpipe, crowding his body as close as possible to reduce the force of anything the guy could throw at him. Ruiz heaved and tried to throw him off. He scrabbled at the hands closed like an iron band around his neck. He kneed, he swung, he tried to butt, but his world was already going dark. Bolan kept up the pressure until the muscled form went limp. When the blood vessels beating wildly beneath his thumbs finally stilled, he relaxed his grasp and got to his feet.

The Mercedes was parked behind a tumble of huge boulders, under the lip of what must once have been a small quarry. He took out the coolie head, closed the trunk quietly and dragged the body out of sight behind the rocks. Then he stole to the edge of the rock pile. It was time for a swift recon.

The short, subtropical twilight was almost over. He saw a bleak upland plain surrounded by a rim of tree-covered hills. The hundred yards of scrub separated the quarry from a tumbledown cabin with shuttered windows through which slits of light showed. Behind the cabin two small sedans were parked next to the canvas-topped truck he'd seen on the customs quay; in front of it a double line of battery-operated red lights stretched across the grassy plateau in the form of a rough flare path. Off to his right, where the dirt road twisted up through a pass, the lights of the coast twinkled in the distance.

Bolan decided to play his hunch through to the end. He had already covered his garish shirt with the denim jacket Ruiz had been wearing. Now he lowered the pagoda hat with its bucolic face over his head and hurried down toward the shack.

Ortiz and three other men were crouched behind the last line of bushes. "What the hell kept you, Ruiz?" the Colombian growled as Bolan approached. "Mannering's due any minute, and the flyboy, too. We've got to get in there first, as soon as Paco gives us the signal."

"How do we know the two of them will be on time?" one of the other men asked before Bolan needed to fake a reply.

"Don't be so stupid," Ortiz snapped. "This is a sensitive operation. They can only rely on so much cooperation from the Dominicans. They want the stuff out of here twice as fast as lightning. The pilot will be on time because he's taking off on a flight plan that's been filed, supposedly on a trip to Nassau, from the airport at Boca Chica, on the other side of Santo Domingo. And that's less than twenty miles away. He's got to stay on time, too, so he can show more or less on schedule at Nassau, after he dumps the load on the cay.''

''Paco tells us this guy Mannering wears this mask when he shows,'' another man muttered. ''What the hell for?''

''So the pilot doesn't recognize him. They only contacted by phone so far. The guy's well-known, so he's crazy on anonymity until his new ID sticks.''

''Crazy is right,'' the fourth man agreed. ''A real nut case!''

''Shut up. I think I hear the plane,'' Ortiz said.

Bolan had heard it too, the drone of a piston-engined aircraft flying in low over the hilltops. He saw the navigation lights against the dark sky, then two brilliant floods that swept over the grass as the plane sideslipped, touched down between the flares, bounced and finally stopped fifty yards from the cabin. The propellers feathered, wheezed and stopped.

''Jesus,'' one of the Colombians whispered. ''You see what that is? It's a B-25, a Mitchell! Those kites were out of date in Korea! You expect us to fly in that?''

A dark figure jumped down from the wing of the twin-engined plane and headed for the cabin.

''It'll have an airworthiness certificate, or the damn thing wouldn't be flying,'' Ortiz grated. ''Now quit complaining and get going. Make it to your places. Ruiz, take the rear entrance. Come in just before Mannering quits his car. He should be on the way up now.''

He paused, listening. From below the pass, they could hear the growl of a powerful automobile in first gear climbing the road that led to the plateau. "Paco's going to step outside to take a leak," Ortiz added. "That's the signal for the rest of you to bust in, while they're still reeling from finding out Ruiz isn't Mannering! Okay?"

Bolan heard murmurs of assent. The gunners moved away through the bushes, and he walked toward the parked cars and the truck. The detonator and the plastic explosives—in two separate one-pound packages—were stowed in the pockets of the denim jacket.

He was approaching the vehicles when the first flicker of brightness swept the sky above the pass. He was behind the truck when the headlight beams swung around again, a little higher, a little brighter, as Mannering's car took the next turn.

The Colombians were wise to Mannering's plan, not only in general but right down to this specific consignment and its split-second timing details. His "leak" looked more like a flood. Who was Paco, the guy on the inside who betrayed his boss? Whoever he was, he had to be someone very close to the American, somebody he trusted and would never suspect. It was ironic that "taking a leak" should signal the double cross.

Ortiz and his men aimed to take out Mannering, hijack the consignment and strong-arm the pilot into flying them out. It was a prize worth fighting for.

The packing cases were of different sizes, but Bolan reckoned they'd average out around six feet long by twenty inches wide. The hidden compartments were five inches deep. Average contents: 7,200 cubic inches. Multiply by the number of cases that remained, forty-seven, and the figure rose to 338,000 cubic inches, or

195 cubic feet. He'd worked that out with Brognola on the carrier.

With almost two hundred cubic feet of merchandise, the truck should be loaded. Bolan whipped the throwing knife from his ankle holster and slashed the nylon cord lacing together the flaps in back of the truck's canvas top. He shone his penlight inside. The packages of cocaine had been stuffed into burlap sacks—and, yeah, they crammed the space to the roof.

BRIGHT LIGHT STROKED the wooden walls of the cabin as the approaching car breasted the saddle at the top of the pass and headed for the strip. It was time Bolan stepped up to bat in place of Ruiz.

There was a door at the top of three steps in the rear wall of the cabin. He unbuttoned the denim jacket, pressed down the latch and walked inside.

The single room was lighted by an oil lamp perched on a rusted stove. Five men stood around a table—Felix, Mexican Ring, two other terrorists Bolan knew by sight, and a lean, hard-bitten, wiry little guy he assumed to be the pilot. Stacks of hundred-dollar bills filled a small attaché case that lay open on the table.

The five heads turned to stare at the grotesque coolie mask disguising the man who came through the door. "Hi, boss," Felix said. "Dead on time as usual, huh?"

"Better be," the pilot snapped. "We gotta hustle, loading this shit, if I have to drop it and make Nassau before they send out a plane missing signal."

"Okay, let's make it," Felix said, looking questioningly at the new arrival. "Okay, boss?"

"Right," Bolan agreed in what he hoped was Mannering's voice. He could hear footsteps on the stony ground outside, and he turned toward the door.

A sudden gush of cool air filled the room as Mexican Ring opened one of two shuttered French doors on the far side of the table. "Where the hell are you going, Paco?" Felix growled.

"Have to take a leak," Paco replied.

"Jesus, you choose your fucking time!" Felix turned back toward the main door, and Paco slipped outside. Bolan reached for the door handle.

The door opened and an identical figure, the same height, wearing an identical mask, walked into the cabin.

Mannering fell back a pace. The men around the table uttered exclamations of astonishment. The pilot gave a snort of laughter. Felix had time to shout an obscenity before the second French door burst open and the burly, bearded Ortiz crashed in with his three confederates and Paco. All of them had drawn guns.

Flame spit briefly from the muzzle in a single short racketing burst as one of the terrorists' hands dived for a hip holster. A 9 mm deathstream slammed the guy back against the table with blood spurting from his savaged chest. The rickety table collapsed beneath his lifeless weight. "That's to show we mean business," Ortiz yelled through the blue smoke. "Now back against the wall, the rest of you bastards, hands behind your heads. *Move!*" He turned to the Executioner. "Ruiz, take their weapons. And you can get rid of that mask now."

Felix, the pilot and the remaining hijacker turned to face the wall while Bolan frisked them. Mannering pulled off his Chinese mask. He was gazing in disbelief at Paco. *"You?"* he choked. "Why, you dirty little..." Words failed him. "But why?"

"Because you're a cheapskate, Mannering." Mexican Ring bit off the words furiously. "Those kids tunneling the mountain for five bucks. You offered them ten—ten lousy bucks—for working nights, doing twice the work. Big fucking deal. Mustn't spoil the market, you said. Well, you sure spoiled the goddamn market for me . . . old pal. Because money's what it's all about, right? And Raul here's paying me twice what you offer—just like you and the kids—plus a percentage on this consignment."

"Not anymore," Ortiz said. "You just outlived your usefulness . . . old pal." The barrel of the Uzi lined up on the traitor who had sold Mannering's secrets. Paco's jaw dropped, his mouth wide open in horror. Ortiz shot him between the teeth. The slugs took away most of his face, dropped him instantly and left an ugly stain of blood and brain tissue on the wall.

Bolan had collected Browning pistols from Felix and the other terrorist, a nickel-plated revolver from the pilot and Mannering's Combat Master. "Okay, stack them on the stove," Ortiz ordered. "I said take off the damned mask, Ruiz. It gives me the fucking creeps."

Bolan hesitated. His hands were full of weaponry. His own two guns were ready in their rigs. But the Uzi was pointing his way, and the other three Colombians all held automatics. Those were sucker odds. It was better—and, hopefully, healthier—to wait.

"Take it *off*!" Ortiz shouted. Then he added suspiciously, "Why don't you speak to me, Ruiz?" His face dropped to the Executioner's bare feet.

"Ruiz was wearing olive drab combat boots!" he growled. "Drop those irons. Hands in the air!"

The Uzi snout was three feet from Bolan's chest. He let the guns drop. Ortiz jerked his head at one of his men. "Damien, take off his mask and frisk him."

The man obeyed. And this time he found the knife. He stood behind Bolan and lifted off the coolie head.

"Belasko!" Mannering exclaimed.

"You again!" Ortiz screamed. "Well, this time I'm going to make sure it's the last time. You and your friend are going to stay here in the dust while we take the consignment and put it where it belongs. That goes for the others, too."

"Look," the pilot said over his shoulder, "this doesn't have anything to do with me. I'm just the hired help. I got no place—"

"Oh, yes, you have, buddy," Ortiz interrupted. "You're the guy who's going to fly us to Colombia once we deck these creeps. You still got plenty to do, believe me!"

Mannering said, "Maybe we could do a deal."

"Oh, sure," Ortiz sneered.

"That's a big consignment, worth one hell—"

"We already got the consignment. We don't need your help now."

"Take Belasko. He's just muscle. But I can give you details of a whole distribution network, producers, outlets, contacts among the Viets . . ."

"Forget it. We're putting the goddamned Viets out of business. Friends of mine stateside have the goods on the Viets. We don't need your network."

Bolan glanced at the watch on the wrist of his raised left hand. It shouldn't be long now. Thirty seconds.

"His name isn't Belasko," Damien said suddenly. "It's Mack Bolan."

"Bolan!" The name exploded simultaneously from Mannering, Ortiz and another of the Colombians. "Sure it is," Damien said. "I ran into the son of a bitch in Florida, a while back, when I was helping out one of the Families. They'll sure give you a big thank-you if you blow *that* one away!"

"Bolan?" Mannering repeated. "But I thought—"

"Life's full of surprises," the Executioner said. *Ten seconds.*

"Here's one for *you*, friend," Ortiz growled, leveling the Uzi at Bolan's chest.

"Be my guest," Bolan said, "if you can shoot that straight."

Ortiz compressed his lips, then shifted his weapon fractionally.

The blast when it came was thunderous, earth-shattering. The wooden cabin disintegrated in a maelstrom of fire.

The two packs of plastique that Bolan had plunged in among the cocaine shipment blew the truck and its cargo to hell. The explosion fired the parked cars, lifted off the roof of the cabin and smashed in the wall.

Bolan had dived to the floor half a hairbreadth before the second hand of his watch indicated zero hour. If Ortiz had pressed the trigger of the Uzi, the sound was lost in the blast.

Now the warrior lay facedown amid a litter of splintered boards. Because he'd been expecting the detonation, he was the first to recover, shake the ringing from his ears and make it to his feet.

He leaped toward the iron stove, which lay on its side by the smashed oil lamp, and snatched the Desert Eagle from the floor. A quick glance left and right filled him in.

The roof had vanished, leaving only a tangle of rafters between the cabin and the stars. The windows had gone and the French doors gaped open. Where the front wall had been there was now a jagged hole beyond which the gutted truck and the three cars flamed fiercely.

In the pulsating red light Bolan saw that the pilot was unconscious, lying on his back beyond the stove with the flue, which had been connected to an outside chimney, resting across his chest. Mannering was dead. A sliver of wood, four feet long and spear-tipped, had penetrated his back between the shoulder blades. The bloodied point protruded from his chest.

Remembering childhood horror stories of vampires killed by a stake driven through the heart—and knowing the man's vile trade—Bolan decided it was a fitting end.

He whirled around, hearing a clatter of wood. Felix, throwing off sections of the pulverized wall, was struggling to his feet with a Colt automatic in his hand. Ignoring Bolan, he continued his private, anticartel war, mercilessly gunning down the two Colombians who had accompanied Ortiz, both of them still dazedly trying to shake off the effects of the blast. As they fell, he turned the gun on Bolan.

The Executioner shot him dead. Not only was he defending himself—he'd seen the man murder an innocent passenger aboard the cruise liner in cold blood, and he'd certainly been implicated in the killing of the steward Flanagan.

Bolan lowered the Desert Eagle. The wrecked cabin was a charnel house of corpses. Of the eleven men who had come, one way or another, to the improvised airstrip, six were dead. The seventh casualty, the last of the

Mannering team, had been smashed over the head by a huge chunk of wood blown from above the door by the explosion. Damien, the third Ortiz gunner, was lying in a far corner, horribly mutilated by the blast.

Of Ortiz there was no sign.

Bolan walked over to the injured hood. There was nothing he could do. Blood was spurting across the dusty floor from the shoulder where an arm had been blown off. There was no place to put a tourniquet. The man would bleed to death within minutes.

Damien's glazed eyes flickered upward, widening momentarily in recognition. "Finish it, soldier," he croaked. "No fuckin' good to anyone like this... Help me... Make it quick."

Bolan fired a mercy round.

Splinters flew from the side wall of the cabin and his ears rang with the hammering blast of submachine gun burst as he straightened and stepped back. He swung around in a combat crouch, the Desert Eagle in his two hands.

Ortiz, blown out through the French doors by the concussion of the blast, was back in the game, his Uzi ready to mow the big man down. In the pulsating light of the flames, Bolan saw that the man's face was a mask of hate. The features twisted into a grimace of glee as he pressed the trigger.

A single loud click told him the SMG's magazine was exhausted.

With a bellow of pure rage, Ortiz rushed forward and swung the Uzi at Bolan's head, following it up with a kick to the crotch that the solder only just avoided by twisting aside.

Bolan flattened his hand and scythed a blow upward that momentarily paralyzed the Colombian's wrist and sent the Uzi flying.

Ortiz came back snarling, and they traded a series of punches.

The combatants grappled with each other, then fell to the ground.

At first, as they fought, the bearded man gained. Astride Bolan's chest, he circled steel hands around his throat, numbing the muscles on each side of the neck, pressing murderously against the windpipe.

The Executioner gagged, fighting for air. A dark mist dimmed the flames. He jammed the heel of one hand beneath the beard, forcing the Colombian's head up and back.

Ortiz gasped through jammed-together teeth. Bolan jerked his hips and swung up his legs, scissoring his ankles around the man's head. Twisting violently then, he tipped the drug dealer sideways, broke the grip on his throat and jumped to his feet to confront his enemy.

There followed an explosion of activity. Feet scrabbled, fists flailed, hoarse cries punctuated the rasps of tortured breath—and finally Ortiz was facedown with the Executioner kneeling on his back. He groaned, heaving wildly, but Bolan's hands were linked beneath his chin, dragging his head up against the agonizing pressure of a knee grinding into the small of his back.

Bolan leaned back with all his weight, arm muscles corded, the sweat pouring from his forehead. A sudden crack signaled that it was over. The Colombian's body went as limp as a deflated balloon.

Bolan lowered Ortiz to the wooden floor and pushed himself groggily to his feet. He looked across the corpse-strewn floor at the pilot. The guy sat among a windfall of hundred-dollar bills, raking in those that weren't charred. The burning drapes had fired part of the wooden wall; soon the whole place would be ablaze.

"That's dirty money," Bolan growled. "Let it burn."

"Hell, I was hired to do a job," the man complained. "It isn't my fault that I couldn't finish it."

"How much were they paying you?"

"Five grand."

The Desert Eagle was back in Bolan's hand. "Take it, and no more. Let the rest burn."

While the pilot counted out bills, the Executioner gazed through the hole where the back wall had been. One of the cars lay on its side with the tires burning, the hood of another looked as though it had been punched by a giant fist, the third had no truck or rear axle. Nothing remained of the truck but a twisted, blackened chassis frame and three wheels. Through the open French doors, Bolan could see that the ancient B-25 was undamaged. He could hear the sound of police sirens. "Could you put that plane down on an aircraft carrier?" he asked.

"I could put her down anywhere."

"I STILL DON'T understand about the ship," Bolan said to Brognola. "I know I heard automatic fire before they left. Then she headed out to sea. What was all that about?"

The big Fed sighed. He shook his head tiredly. "Bastards shot the captain, the first officer, the engineer chief, helmsman—anyone who could identify Mannering and put him among the hijackers," he said. "Then they just aimed her at the horizon and split. We put a squad of marines aboard finally, but there were no terrorists left to fight. All the guys had to do was unlock doors and let the passengers out!''

"Nice people."

The Fed nodded. "Efficient, too." He pushed a fax toward Bolan. A smudged newsprint clipping from a paper published in Bogotá reported that a certain Captain Fernandez of the Medellín police department, lately transferred from Criminal Investigation to traffic duty, had been shot dead by two unknown assailants.

Bolan sighed. "At least I was able to recover the contact lists and file cards from Mannering's body," he said. "That should give the narcotics team a handle on some of the dishonest cops."

"Some of them," Brognola agreed.

"But there's still one thing that puzzles the hell out of me."

"Namely?"

"What did Mannering say to Ortiz—an enemy, a guy on the other side of the fence—that made him call off his gorillas when I jumped out of their car?"

"You'll never know," Brognola said. "All we do know is that there is no honor among thieves. You get cross, double cross and triple cross when this kind of money is involved. Always have, always will."

"I guess so," the Executioner said somberly. "You hope maybe the rivals might cancel each other out. But it never happens."

He rose from the carrier's wardroom table and stretched. "That's why the battle has to go on."

"Some of the most riveting war fiction written..."
—Ed Gorman, *Cedar Rapids Gazette*

VIETNAM: GROUND ZERO.

SNIPER

ERIC HELM

The Vietnam War rages on as Special Forces Captain Mack Gerber embarks on his latest order—to assassinate top Red Chinese officials planning PLA troop protection of the Ho Chi Minh Trail.

Charlie, Gerber's nineteen-year-old hit man, is a talented sniper with twenty confirmed kills in only two months of service, but the kid has a conscience and it's got Gerber worried. Charlie's up against the best sniper in the People's Army and it only takes one shot to change things for good.

Available now at your favorite retail outlet, or order your copy by sending your name, address, zip or postal code along with a check or money order for $5.25 (includes 75¢ postage and handling) payable to Gold Eagle Books to:

In the U.S.
Gold Eagle Books
901 Fuhrmann Blvd.
Box 1325
Buffalo, NY 14269-1325

In Canada
P.O. Box 609
Fort Erie, Ontario
L2A 5X3

Please specify book title with your order.

SVGZ5-1A

ABLE TEAM ®
DICK STIVERS

Check out the action in two ABLE TEAM books you won't find in stores anywhere!

Don't miss out on these two riveting adventures of ABLE TEAM, the relentless three-man power squad:

DEATH HUNT—Able Team #50 $2.95 ☐
The lives of 20 million people are at stake as Able Team plays
hide-and-seek with a warped games master.

SKINWALKER—Able Team #51 $2.95 ☐
A legendary Alaskan werewolf has an appetite for local Eskimos
fighting a proposed offshore drilling operation.

Total Amount	$ _____
Plus 75¢ Postage	.75
Payment enclosed	$ _____

Please send a check or money order payable to Gold Eagle Books.

In the U.S.
901 Fuhrmann Blvd.
P.O. Box 1325
Buffalo, NY 14269-1325

In Canada
P.O. Box 609
Fort Erie, Ontario
L2A 5X3

Please Print
Name: _____
Address: _____
City: _____
State/Province: _____
Zip/Postal Code: _____

GOLD
EAGLE ®

ATD-1

Do you know a real hero?

At Gold Eagle Books we know that heroes are not just fictional. Everyday someone somewhere is performing a selfless task, risking his or her own life without expectation of reward.

Gold Eagle would like to recognize America's local heroes by publishing their stories. If you know a true to life hero (that person might even be you) we'd like to hear about him or her. In 150-200 words tell us about a heroic deed you witnessed or experienced. Once a month, we'll select a local hero and award him or her with national recognition by printing his or her story on the inside back cover of THE EXECUTIONER series, and the ABLE TEAM, PHOENIX FORCE and/or VIETNAM: GROUND ZERO series.

Send your name, address, zip or postal code, along with your story of 150-200 words (and a photograph of the hero if possible), and mail to:

LOCAL HEROES AWARD
Gold Eagle Books
225 Duncan Mill Road
Don Mills, Ontario
M3B 3K9
Canada